NO
ESCAPE

NO ESCAPE

MAREN STOFFELS

TRANSLATED BY LAURA WATKINSON

UNDERLINED

Text copyright © 2022 by Maren Stoffels
Cover art used under license from Shutterstock.com
Translation copyright © 2024 by Laura Watkinson

Underlined is a registered trademark and the colophon is a trademark of Penguin Random House LLC.

GetUnderlined.com

Educators and librarians, for a variety of teaching tools, visit us at RHTeachersLibrarians.com

Library of Congress Cataloging-in-Publication Data is available upon request.
ISBN 978-0-593-70877-4 (pbk.) — ISBN 978-0-593-70878-1 (ebook)

The text of this book is set in 12-point Sabon Next.
Interior design by Ken Crossland

Printed in the United States of America
3rd Printing
First American Edition

For all my readers worldwide who were so
enthusiastic about my book *Escape Room*.
You urged me to go on a new adventure in
an extreme escape room. Thank you.

And also for Eva,
who is just as much a fan
of escape rooms as I am.
I think we're friends. ;)

CASE nr. 1999-5

E. Shepherd—psychiatrist

OBSERVATION:

What immediately strikes me is that the girl looks completely feral. Her nails are black. There are bloodstains on her fingers and clothes. Her hair hangs limply around her face. Her eyes are darting back and forth.

She's constantly fiddling with her black necklace.

When the police officer asks her if she might like to change her clothes and holds out a hand to her, the girl completely freaks out.

<u>She is making animal noises.</u>

When I'm allowed to talk to the girl, after an hour and a half, she's sitting on the floor in a corner of the room. She appears to have calmed down.

The girl doesn't respond when I ask her if she

knows who I am and what I'm doing there. When I ask her what her name is, she just stares at her hands.

I introduce myself to her, tell her I'm a psychiatrist and that she can call me Edward Shepherd.

I decide to take a gamble and ask her what she was doing in that isolated place.

The girl just presses her back against the wall.

I tell her I understand that it's hard to talk about the situation, but it's important that she does.

This time, much to my surprise, the girl says something.

"Sorry, but you'll never understand. No one knows what it was like in there."

THIS
IS
WHERE
THE
TEAMS
ARE
FORMED

LEXI

The train emerges from the darkness.

There are no crossing gates here, just a fence to keep people off the tracks. But I searched around and found a spot where I could get through.

I'm standing with the toes of my sneakers against the steel track. If I concentrate, I can feel the vibration in my body. The train is approaching.

I close my eyes and, for a moment, everything is sharp.

The cry of an owl somewhere nearby, the scent of the pine trees alongside the railroad tracks, the taste of tonight's spaghetti still in my mouth. I can even follow the path my blood is taking through my body.

The vibration is getting stronger.

Less than thirty seconds to go.

Less than ten seconds.

I can see the driver, but can he see me too? It's so dark here.

What if he doesn't notice me?

Finally—there's the horn.

It's so loud that it's like someone is holding a megaphone next to my ear.

I take a big step back.

Less than five seconds later, I feel the blast of the train. It doesn't push me away, but it sucks me in, as if the train is still going to devour me after all.

I tense all my muscles, bracing myself. One by one, the train cars thunder by, like a pounding headache.

I don't open my eyes again until the last car has gone by.

The train's red taillights are swiftly disappearing into the distance.

I laugh. I can't help myself. Out loud, as if someone just told a really good joke.

I felt that.

I felt all of it.

With a sigh of relief, I turn and walk back to the fence.

When I've squeezed through the gap, I carefully put the wire back in place.

I climb up to the overpass, where my bike is leaning against a lamppost. And that's when I notice someone standing beside it.

Startled, I still. *What's going on?* There's never anyone else here—that's exactly why I chose this spot.

What if they saw me and called the police? Then I'm

probably going to get a load of questions. They'll have the completely wrong idea.

But the woman by my bike doesn't appear to have seen me. She's taking something out of her pocket and leaning over my handlebars.

"Hey!" I yell. "What are you doing?"

The woman looks up, startled, but then her bright red lips form a small smile, as if she recognizes me.

Who is she? I'm sure I've never seen her before.

Before I can react, she runs off, her high heels tapping along the overpass.

For a moment, I think about going after her, and then I notice something sticking out of my bell. It's a white business card.

I take the card and look up. The woman has already reached the other end of the overpass. She gets into a car and drives away.

On one side of the card, there's a telephone number, and on the other side, written in bloodred letters, it says: *TIME FOR A LITTLE ESCAPE?*

I look in the direction the woman went. Does she think I want to buy drugs? Because this has to be some kind of direct line to a dealer. What else could it be?

She couldn't have chosen a worse candidate. Ever since Tess's diagnosis, I've hated pills of every kind.

I take my phone from my pocket and key in the number. It rings three times and then someone picks up.

"Hello?" says a stranger's voice.

"You left your business card," I say. "I'm not a junkie. Okay? And I don't know what you think you just saw, but I wasn't trying to kill myself."

For a moment I think about Kelly. She must have been so scared.

"I'm not desperate. So leave me alone."

"Say your name."

Huh? My name?

"Lexi," I say hesitantly.

"Hello, Lexi. Who's your best friend?"

The voice sounds strange, nothing like a woman's voice. But not like a man's voice either. More like a robot, as if I'm talking to a computer.

"My best friend?"

I pause, maybe because so much has changed between Tess and me. Since Kelly's death, our friendship has been on shaky ground, like it could collapse at any moment.

But I still know there's only one answer to this question.

"My best friend's name is Tess," I say, clearly picturing my cousin. Her green eyes, which suddenly seemed as dark as night after Kelly's suicide. Tess's eyes were like ringing crossing gates, warning that the Shadow was coming.

Why didn't I see it?

But I thought Tess was mourning the girl who lived next door.

My aunt thought the same. We didn't see the Shadow until it was almost too late.

"Lexi and Tess. You will be expected at Escape Room 2.0 on Saturday, March thirteenth, at two p.m. The address is two-sixty-two Industry Road. Wishing you a pleasant escape!"

And the line goes dead.

BEAU

"So you're telling me some complete stranger spoke to you on Thursday after the concert? And she gave you a business card?"

Zora and I are cycling to Industry Road. There's a strong wind, and I'm struggling to keep up with her.

I nod. "You've asked me that three times now. Red just suddenly turned up behind Club 7."

The alley behind the concert hall was the only place where I could catch my breath. There were no fans there, and Benji didn't know where to look for me.

But then that woman suddenly showed up. In my mind, she's called Red, because she was dressed head to toe in that color.

"But that's really bizarre, isn't it?" Zora glances across at me. "What else did this Red say to you?"

"Not much. She just said it was a special kind of escape room."

"And you have no idea who she is?" Zora doesn't seem to be bothered by the wind. She's pedaling away like it's no effort at all.

"No," I say. "Not a clue."

"It's not some deranged fan, is it?"

I shake my head. "She didn't look the type."

I picture Red, with her lipstick and those red high heels. At first, I thought she was a scout from a modeling agency, but then she started talking about the escape room. She said it was completely different than other escape rooms. This is Escape Room 2.0, and it's "no ordinary escape room," whatever that's supposed to mean.

"I can't believe Benji just let you leave today." Zora stands up on her pedals. "Your studio time is sacred."

"I'm going into the studio tomorrow."

I think about the phone conversation I just had. I was surprised that Benji agreed to my time off too, but then he told me the big news.

Los Angeles.

LA wants *me*.

My armpits start sweating. My family is going to flip when they hear about this.

Grandpa always said that one day I'd play New York's Madison Square Garden, one of the most famous venues in the world.

When we visited him there last year, he bought basketball tickets, and we sat way up at the very top.

I felt so tiny and huge at the same time. Just the thought that I might get to sing there one day . . . wow!

When I got back home, I really went for it. I did even more interviews, performances, and meet-and-greets.

And just now, Benji told me that it all paid off. Next month we're flying to LA to meet with a real-life label and sign a contract.

I glance across at Zora. Why haven't I told her yet?

Because then I'd have to tell her about all my doubts.

And then I'd have to explain why.

For a moment, I'm back at the intersection.

Mariposa.

Her name was stuck to the inside of my head, like a sticky note. Mariposa. The Spanish word for *butterfly*.

That moment in September, my singing instantly faded into the background.

For months, I refused to perform. I couldn't even sing in the shower.

How could I sing?

Thursday was my first performance in months, but it felt too soon. Way too soon.

"Is this really it?" Zora asks as we take a left turn.

The wind suddenly blasts right into our faces. My skin feels like a pincushion, stinging with the cold.

"This is Industry Road," I say. We're only at number one. Looks like we have a way to go yet.

A car drives past. Then brakes. The passenger window goes down.

"Hey, Beau!" A guy is looking at me. "You're Beau!"

My heart skips a beat. Even here, in *the middle of nowhere*, people recognize me.

"Beauuuuu!" comes the cry from the back seat. The way they say my name is so hysterical that they sound like a bunch of preschoolers. But it's three guys crammed in next to each other. They're all doing my captain's salute. I did that at a photo shoot once, tapping an invisible cap with my first two fingers. Benji loved it—and it became my trademark.

" '*Love is nothing but trouble, nothing but pain. Hope I'll see you . . . ,* '" the guy in the front sings, holding out an imaginary microphone to me.

" '*Never again,*' " I sing back reluctantly.

"Good job, dude!" The boy sticks his thumb up.

"Your songs are junk, but they're catchy. My girlfriend is totally in love with you."

"That's nice," I say, pedaling faster.

But he's not done yet. The car is still driving alongside me.

"Okay if I take a quick picture of you?" Without waiting for an answer, he leans out of the open window and takes a selfie. I don't even have time to look into the camera.

"Hey, what are you actually doing out here, bro?"

Dude. Bro. People always act like they know me, but they

don't. They just recognize me—and that's something else entirely.

"We're going to an escape room," Zora says when I don't reply.

"Oh, sweet." He looks back at his friends. "They got one out here?"

"Just down the road," I say. "It's called Escape Room 2.0."

"Sounds good. We'll check it out. Have fun, bro!" He raises the window again.

Just before they speed off around the corner, they give me a blast of their horn.

When they're out of sight, I hear Zora chuckle to herself.

"My girlfriend is totally in love with you. . . ." She sounds exactly like the guy we just spoke to.

"Shut up."

"Oh, come on. That was hilarious, wasn't it?" Zora says, hitting her handlebars. "And what did you say? *'That's nice.'*"

She can imitate even my deep voice perfectly. I remember this one time when Zora phoned a girl for me because I was too chicken. She said she'd get me a date—and she did.

A moment later, I squeeze my brakes. "This is it." We'd almost gone past the gray building, but I saw the number just in time: 262.

We lock up our bikes and walk to the two doors, which are right next to each other. There are red lights above them. Is this the entrance? But which of the two doors is the right one?

I point at the sign beside the door on the right. Written in the same bloodred letters as on the business card: *ESCAPE ROOM 2.0.*

But when Zora tries to open the door, it won't budge. The other door is locked too.

This is a bit weird, isn't it? I check my phone—but I got the time right.

"Maybe we should ring the bell?" Zora says, pointing at the intercom.

"Go on, then." I blow into my cupped hands to warm them. "It's so cold out here."

Just as Zora is about to press the bell, I hear a voice behind me.

"So you're the ones we're up against?"

LEXI

Doing this escape room is either my best plan ever—or my worst one.

As I look at Tess cycling along beside me, I know this could go one of two ways. Up or down. Sink or swim.

What if this is a really bad plan?

"Did you take your pills?" I ask, just to make sure.

"Of course," Tess says with a sigh. "You sound like Mom."

I bite the inside of my cheek. Since the onset of Tess's depression, I often sound like that. Like I don't know how to simply be Lexi anymore. I feel like I need to watch my words all the time.

Tess is leaning over her handlebars. I can see her roots on top of her head, where the black dye has finally given way to her natural hair color. I hated that she dyed it. We both have bright red hair, like our moms.

We turn left. This is Industry Road. We're only at number one.

"Mom thinks I don't take them on purpose."

I look at her. "Why would you do that?"

"Because they make me so sleepy."

"Yes, but anything's better than . . ." *The Shadow,* I think, but I never say that word out loud. Just like I never ask Tess anymore how she slept, how she feels, or if she's had a good day.

"I don't feel that terrible anymore," says Tess. "But I don't feel great either. Know what I mean?"

I nod, but I have no idea what that kind of thing feels like. We used to be like twins, just like our moms, but now it's sometimes like we live in two different worlds.

"Did you see that suicide story on the news yesterday?" Tess says, glancing across at me. "They mentioned Kelly again."

Kelly. Every time Tess mentions her name, I flinch.

"I don't watch the news" is all I say, hoping Tess will drop the subject, but she just keeps talking.

"They started going on again about her being a victim of bullying and that her friends joined in with it. Seriously, they're still calling them her friends! How can they say they . . ."

Tess's voice falters. I know the story. Just about everyone knows about Kelly, because it was such a tragedy.

I can still hear my mom and dad saying, *Such a pretty young girl, and with such a wonderful future ahead of her.*

But that pretty young girl decided one day that there was no way she could carry on.

"She never should have gone to that other high school." Tess is cycling faster and faster. "She should have gone with us. Then she'd never have met those girls."

I know Tess can go around in circles endlessly when it comes to Kelly.

"They interviewed some psychiatrist too. Some guy named Shepherd. He does a lot of stuff with EMDR therapy."

"A lot of what?"

"It stands for Eye Movement Desensitization and Reprocessing. It's a form of therapy that gets you to revisit the most traumatic part of your memory. Gradually it reduces the strength of the trauma."

The terminology makes my head spin. Sometimes Tess talks like she's years older than me, even though there's only a day between us.

"He seems really good," Tess continues. "Maybe he could have helped Kelly."

"We don't know that," I reply.

"Shepherd says that people often sound the alarm too late." Tess bites her lip. "That's the problem. That people don't ask for help soon enough."

When Tess ran away from home, I thought it was too late as well. I was sure we were going to lose her, like Kelly.

"It's not fair. That Kelly's not alive anymore, but I am," says Tess.

"You can't think like that." My voice cracks. "You heard what the doctor said, didn't you? She made a decision in a moment of panic. No one could have prevented that. No one."

Tess is silent.

What's she thinking now? I always used to know what was on her mind, but now I just have to guess.

"Are you . . . are you sure you want to go to this escape room?"

Tess brakes and gets off her bike. "What do you mean?"

"Because it . . ."

Because it's my worst plan ever?

I lied to my aunt and said I was taking Tess into town for a movie. Lonnie even gave us twenty dollars!

If I'd mentioned the escape room, she'd never have let her daughter go. I'm sure of it. The doctor says Tess needs to increase her activities slowly.

But I want the old Tess back. Maybe that'll happen if we do the sort of stuff we used to do before.

"Because it's all . . . kind of mysterious?" I think about the strange woman who left the card and about the robotic voice on the phone.

"Hey, but mysteries are cool. And we'll be together, won't we?"

"Yes, but . . ."

"You met the owner, didn't you?"

"Well, not exactly. I only saw her."

"And you called that number."

"Yes."

"On that prehistoric phone of yours."

"Hey, it still works just fine."

Tess smiles. I don't think she's done that for weeks. "So, let's get going, okay?"

"Yes, but . . ."

"Come on. What are you trying to say?"

I hesitate. "Maybe it's too much?"

"Stop it, Lex," Tess says, slowly and calmly. "Stop playing babysitter."

I want to say that I don't mean it like that, but Tess jumps back onto her bike and rides off. I struggle to keep up with her.

Lonnie's voice echoes through my mind.

You will keep an eye on Tess, won't you? she had said. *If anything feels off, then you guys come back home. Got it?*

If she finds out where we're really going, she'll kill me.

This is my worst plan ever.

Then we're outside number 262. There are two people already waiting.

Tess and I lock up our bikes and walk over to them.

They're trying to open the door and haven't noticed we've arrived.

"So you're the ones we're up against?" I ask, to get their attention.

The boy looks around, startled. Next to me, I hear Tess gasp.

Is she really that impressed? He's not *that* good-looking.

"You guys here for the escape room too?" the girl asks.

I nod. "I'm Lexi and this is Tess."

"Let me guess," says the boy. His voice is so low that the air seems to vibrate. "Best friends?"

"And cousins," I say. "You guys?"

"Not related." The girl gives us a big grin. It's true—they don't look anything like each other. They're opposites, in fact. The girl is small and pale and has straight hair halfway down her back. The boy's tall, with brown skin and a mass of curls.

"I'm Zora," she says. "And this is Beau."

"You called that number?" I ask.

Beau nods. "Some woman told me about it on Thursday night."

Thursday night. Same as me.

"Any idea who she is?" asks Tess.

Beau shakes his head. "No clue. But I call her Red."

Red. I get it. Her lipstick as she gave me that mysterious smile . . .

"Do you think it's legit?" I point at the doors. "It's all a bit creepy, huh?"

"There's a sign up there." Zora nods. "Seems real enough."

I look up. The building has several floors, but there are no windows. It seems to be some kind of business, like so many of the other buildings around here. During the week, people work here, but on weekends it's dead.

"Okay, let's ring the bell," I say. "And if it's lame, we can always leave."

Beau presses the button on the intercom. Part of me hopes it's just one big joke. Then I'll take Tess into town for a movie after all, like I told Lonnie I would.

But there's that robotic voice again, the one I heard when I called the phone number.

"Hello. May I have your names?"

"Beau, Zora, Tess, and Lexi," Beau recites.

"Welcome," the voice continues. *"You have been selected to participate in this new game: Escape Room 2.0."*

I glance at Tess. She's staring intently at the intercom. I take her hand and give it a squeeze.

"This. Is. So. Awesome," she whispers excitedly. For a moment, I see a glimpse of the old Tess, the complete games fanatic.

"Please deposit your personal belongings in the lockbox beside the door."

Now I notice the two slots.

"Telephones, keys, wallets. When you're done, press the button again."

There is silence.

Beau looks back at us. "So I guess we just do as we're told, right?"

"It's all part of the game," says Zora. "There was this one room where I forgot to hand in my phone. And they weren't happy. They're worried you're going to put photos on social media, and then the escape room won't be any fun for new players."

"Lexi's phone isn't a threat," Tess says with a wink.

"Why not?" asks Beau. When I take it out, he laughs. "Wow, where did you get that from?"

"Bought it," I say. "Why?"

"Oh, no reason." Beau tries to keep a straight face. "It's just that it's . . . kind of . . . prehistoric."

Tess grins. "That's what I always tell her!"

"Hey, it works just fine," I say for the second time today.

"I think it's cool." Zora holds the lockbox open for me. "But hand it in anyway."

I hesitate for a moment. I need to be able to contact Lonnie if there's a problem with Tess. What if she has an episode when she's in there?

But then again, I'm not going to leave Tess on her own for a second. Nothing can go wrong if I stay close to her. And she only just took her pills.

An escape room takes, like, an hour to do. And if any-thing does go wrong in there, I can just press the emer-gency button. And that Red woman will open the door for us and let us out.

"Lexi?" Tess urges me after the other three have put their phones in the lockbox.

"Okay." I drop my phone into the slot. The dull thud on the bottom of the lockbox is the signal for Beau to press the buzzer.

The robotic voice speaks again.

"In front of you, there are two doors. The doors are the entrances to two identical escape rooms, one for each team of two."

Tess leans over and whispers to me: "We're going to win."

Her words are like magic—all my doubts disappear. That's what she always used to say whenever we chal-lenged our moms to a game of Pictionary. We never won. Of course we didn't, because you have no chance of winning when you're playing against twins. Our moms are like one person who's been split into two bodies. They think, feel, and talk exactly the same.

But with this game, we do stand a chance. Zora and Beau aren't twins—far from it.

Tess wants to win. Or maybe she just doesn't want to lose for once. Maybe, just maybe, she'll forget the Shadow in there, even if it's only for a few seconds.

Zora and Beau stand in front of the door on the left. Tess and I go for the one on the right.

I can feel my heart pounding against my ribs. What's the room going to be like?

I take a quick look at the others. That Zora seems so competitive. . . . And didn't she say she's done escape rooms before?

"We can beat them," whispers Tess.

"We sure can," I whisper back.

The doctor can say whatever he likes, but he doesn't know Tess. She doesn't want a babysitter, she doesn't want to build things up slowly—no, she wants to throw herself back into life. This escape room is my best plan ever.

"Just one more thing before you head inside." The voice pauses. *"You will not be playing alongside the person you came here with."*

My eyes flash to the intercom. Huh?

"You're going to switch partners. The players who were invited will form a team of two. Your best friends will be your opponents."

BEAU

"No!" the girl named Lexi shouts. She has bright orange hair and more freckles than I can count. "That's bullshit!"

All three of us stare at her.

"Lexi . . . ," begins Tess, but Lexi is turning paler and paler.

"No. No way!"

"It's not a problem. I'm okay with it," Tess says.

"Well, I'm not." Lexi looks at me. "I'm not teaming up with him."

"Nice. Thanks," I say, but Lexi ignores me.

She must be one of the haters. I have almost as many haters as I do fans.

Benji has taught me over the years that I need to develop a thick skin when it comes to people like that, and I'm doing a pretty good job. Whenever they start calling me names, I just smile.

Zora doesn't. She's always sticking up for me online.

Lexi leans forward and speaks into the intercom. "I'm playing with Tess. Or I'm not playing at all."

Why is she being so difficult?

"Follow the rules" is the only reply.

I see Zora looking at me. She's probably not happy about the switch either, but at least she's not freaking out about it.

"What's the problem?" I say. "Why don't we just do what they want? So we're playing against each other instead of together. Big deal."

"Agreed," says Tess. "Come on, Lexi. I want to go inside. It's freezing out here."

Lexi clenches her jaw.

"It's part of the game," I add. "You heard what they said, didn't you?"

Lexi glares at me, her eyes practically burning holes in my skin.

"The point is the escape room, isn't it? Not the teams." Tess smiles and gives her cousin a nudge. "Or are you scared I'm going to beat you?"

There's a brief silence.

For a moment, I'm afraid Lexi is going to turn around and leave. Then we won't have anyone to play against.

I was really looking forward to this escape room. There might be cameras inside, but they're not there for me. In there, I can just be Beau, without having my whole name written in capital letters.

There won't be any fans chasing me around every single moment. My height doesn't help. I'm so tall that I tower above everything.

Inside, there's only one thing that matters: escaping from the room in time.

"Lexi?" Tess wraps her arms around Lexi and I see her whispering something in her ear. I can't hear what she says, but Lexi's face softens.

"Okay," she says as they let go of each other. "We'll swap."

The robotic voice seems to have heard, because the lights above the doors turn green.

"Great." I reach for the handle Zora tried earlier and push it down. This time, the door moves. The space behind it is pitch-black.

I glance at Zora, who has opened her door too.

It feels strange to have her as an opponent. We always do everything together. When a gang of kids from my class was waiting to beat me up in elementary school, she helped me to fight back. Whenever we have a difficult school assignment, I let her copy from me. And she always comes to gigs with me. It's way more fun with her in the back seat.

And now we're suddenly supposed to be competing against each other.

But I don't want to get all dramatic about it like Lexi did, so I give Zora a thumbs-up.

"Good luck."

"You too." Zora glances at Lexi and makes a face. "I think you're going to need it."

I smile. Zora can tell that Lexi's a hater too. Maybe she's left a mean comment under one of my videos. Most of them are along the same lines: *Drop dead, homo. Think you can sing?* and that kind of thing.

Zora does her best to respond to as much as she can, but it's pointless. It doesn't matter how many fans stick up for me. The haters' comments keep on coming. Benji says it's all good. If you want to be a big success, you need the haters too.

The thought of LA flashes through my mind. Mom and Dad don't even know about it yet.

I'll tell them when I get home. I bet Dad goes out and buys a cake to celebrate. And Mom will call the entire family.

The pressure in my chest increases. What if I can't do it? Thursday's show already felt too soon. So how am I supposed to go to LA?

"Good luck, teams. May the best players win."

"Are you coming?" Zora says to Tess.

"Hang on." Lexi puts her arms around Tess again. Zora rolls her eyes. She hates all that girlie stuff.

Lexi finally lets go of Tess.

I open the door to the escape room wider. "Ladies first."

"I'm not a lady," snaps Lexi. "You can go first."

I smile. Lexi might seem cute with all those freckles and that old-fashioned phone, but she's like a raging wildfire.

I'm the first to step through the door. The room is completely dark. I have no idea what's going on. Where's the reception desk? Or doesn't this place have a reception? Are we already standing in the middle of the escape room? Where's that Red woman? She must be somewhere around here.

"You guys see anything?" I hear Zora ask.

I stick my head around the corner. "No."

"Maybe we need to shut the door behind us first," says Lexi. "And then the lights will come on automatically."

Makes sense.

"Let's do it on three." Zora starts counting: "One, two . . . three!"

And then it really is dark.

For a moment, I'm alone with my breathing.

It's like the silence before a show.

My fans scream nonstop for an hour and a half, but in those few seconds before I begin, they're completely silent.

That's my favorite moment.

A light goes on. Then another, and another. Lexi was right!

I shield my eyes against the bright lights at first, but then I make out a few large objects.

It takes me a moment to realize what they are.

Spread out there under the spotlights are three coffins.

CASE nr. 1999-5

E. Shepherd—psychiatrist

AUDIO RECORDING:

"I'd like to apologize for just now.
You're absolutely right. I don't
understand your situation. The police
have told me a few things about what
happened. It must have been terrible
in there."

  [. . .]

  "So you're a psychiatrist?"

  "Yes, that's right."

  "I'm not crazy."

  "No one thinks you are."

  "So why did they set you on me?"

  "Like I said: I'm here to—"

"What about the others? Shouldn't you be talking to them?"

"If there's a need for that, then yes, but you're the—"

Loud bang.

"Don't you dare finish that sentence!"

"Please sit down."

"Do not call me a victim!"

Someone enters the room.

"Everything okay here, Shepherd?"

"No, fuck off! You guys have no idea what I went through. It's the other three you should be talking to! Why am I here while they . . . Hey, let go of me. Let me go. LET. ME. G—"

The recording stops.

THIS
IS
WHEN
THE
DOOR
WON'T
OPEN

LEXI

The three caskets are neatly lined up in a row, with floral wreaths on top. It's such a bizarre sight that it takes me a few seconds to realize what I'm looking at. I'd been expecting all kinds of things, but not this. It's like I'm in a funeral home.

Tess . . .

She's in the other room now.

Is she seeing exactly the same thing as I am? I guess she must be, because that robotic voice said the escape rooms are identical.

Why didn't I stay with her?

When she sees these coffins, she's going to lose it. The last casket we saw was Kelly's.

At the funeral, Tess squeezed my hand so hard that it went completely numb. But I kept holding her hand, all through the entire service.

She almost choked on her tears that afternoon when she made her speech. She insisted on saying something, but she could hardly get her words out.

It was horrible to watch.

It was as if Tess developed a hole in her body that day, and the Shadow crept inside her without any difficulty.

And now Tess is sitting in that other room, all on her own. Yeah, Zora's there, but she doesn't know her. Zora has no idea what Tess has been going through these past few months.

You will keep an eye on Tess, won't you?

What if Tess loses it in here? She needs to get out of this place as fast as possible.

I'm about to turn around, but then I see the rest of the room. The walls are made of bricks, there's an elevator door, and, of course, the exit.

Behind the coffins, there's a wall.

A wall made of glass.

And on the other side of it, I see . . .

"Tess!" I run to the glass and bang my fist on it. Tess doesn't look up. She's just staring at the coffins in her own room. It's true—it's an exact copy of ours.

"Tess! Tess! Are you okay?"

My cousin doesn't react. Then the robotic voice echoes around the room.

"You can see the other team, but you can't hear them."

Now Tess looks in my direction. When our eyes meet, she smiles for a moment. She's a bit paler than usual, but otherwise she seems okay.

I watch as she puts her hair up in a ponytail. Tess pulls it extra tight, as if she wants to make sure it stays in place.

The gesture is so familiar that my eyes fill with tears. She always does that before we start playing a game, as if she's preparing for battle.

"There are three coffins in front of you. Your task is to open them and to find out how the people inside them died. Do this carefully because the other team can, of course, copy you. There is only one exit. And that is at the end of this escape room. The team that finds the exit first, wins."

The intercom falls silent.

Open the coffins? What a demented thing to ask us to do!

My gaze returns to Tess. Is she going to be able to handle this?

Tess smiles at me and puts her thumb up. Then she and Zora start searching the room.

Tess is okay.

She really is okay.

I watch her for a little longer, but then I tear my gaze away. I shouldn't worry so much.

She doesn't want a babysitter. She wants her best friend

back. That was exactly what she whispered in my ear before we entered.

She says she doesn't need any more counselors. She's already seen enough of them.

I take a deep breath.

"We're going to win," I whisper at the glass. Even though I'm not Tess's teammate, it still feels like I am. The more I try, the harder she'll work too. And then, just for a while, she'll forget all the other stuff that's happened in the past few months.

I turn around. "Right. Where do we start?"

For the first time since we entered, I see Beau. He's still standing by the door, staring at the coffins as if he expects a corpse to rise out of one of them at any moment.

He's not scared, is he?

"You know it's fake, right?" I remind him.

Beau looks at me. "Huh?"

"It's not real," I add.

"No . . ." Beau shakes his curls back and forth. "I am aware of that, you know."

I point at the first coffin. "This one has a three-digit combination lock. Let's both search the room. Yell if you find something that looks like a code."

I take one last glance at the room next to ours, and then I start searching. I run my hands over the walls. The bricks feel rough under my fingers.

The walls don't appear to be hiding any secrets, so I cross the floor on all fours. Could there be something under the coffins? I check out the space under the tables that the coffins are on. It feels weird crawling beneath them, but I have to do it. If I want to win this game, I've got to do whatever it takes.

There's nothing under the first coffin. I crawl on, but all I find under the second and third is dust. When I stand up again, Beau is still by the entrance. He rattles the door handle.

"This is not an exit," says the robotic voice.

"No way it's going to be that easy," I say. Why isn't Beau helping? Being all chivalrous with his "ladies first"—but now he seems happy to let me do all the work!

I look around. Except for the three coffins, the room is completely empty. It feels strange: usually there are all kinds of things to explore in an escape room.

I walk over to the coffins and inspect the wreaths. I read the words on the ribbons that are attached to them. It's the standard stuff you'd expect to see at a funeral.

" *'Rest in peace, AJ,'* " I read on the first one. "Maybe we need to change the letters of the name into numbers? *A* is one, *B* is two . . . so AJ would be . . . one hundred ten."

But when I key in the code, the lock doesn't open.

Beau is still standing perfectly still by the door. Why

couldn't I be on that Zora's team? At least she appears to be competitive. This Beau guy is no use to me at all.

Does he have claustrophobia? But then you wouldn't sign up for an escape room, would you?

I focus on the numbers again. Three digits—how hard can it be?

I take another look at the first ribbon. What have I missed?

"They've got the coffin open."

I look up and see that Beau is right. Zora and Tess are giving each other a high five and lifting the lid off the first coffin.

I can feel the nerves racing through my body. With a normal escape room, you're battling against the clock, but this is much more nerve-racking. We're behind now, and I have no idea how Zora and Tess managed to open the first coffin.

" 'Rest in peace, AJ,' " I read out loud. " 'Forever in our' . . . Wait a second. . . ." The dates of birth and death are on the back of the ribbon. The date of birth is too long, because 1122 is four digits, but the date of death might . . . "December fourth. That makes it . . . one-two-four." My hands trembling, I key in the digits. This time, the lock clicks open. It feels like my heart does a backflip.

I felt that.

"Done!" I take the lock off the coffin and look over my

shoulder at Beau. He's staring at the coffin as if it's going to open by itself.

I've had enough of this.

"Are you going to help me lift this heavy lid? Or are you just going to stand there and pose, like some wannabe model?"

BEAU

There are three coffins in front of me.

A dark one, a white one, and one made of plain wood. But I can see another one too, one that's not there at all.

A white one, with blue butterflies on it.

Mariposa.

Even in the escape room, she's here.

I can see her coffin in front of me so vividly that it's like I'm back in the funeral home.

I can't breathe.

The pain in my chest is getting worse. It's like my body's splitting in two.

I focus on my breathing, the way Benji once taught me. He says this exercise helps when you're singing, but I often use it offstage too.

"Are you going to help me lift this heavy lid? Or are you just going to stand there and pose, like some wannabe model?"

It takes me a second to realize Lexi is talking to me.

I look at her. "Huh?"

"Never mind!" Lexi is tugging frantically at the lid.

I know I should help her, but I can't.

That Red could have chosen any theme at all, so why did she choose death? This is so . . . sick.

Red's words echo inside my head. *This is no ordinary escape room.*

What did she actually mean? That it's completely realistic?

I look at the exit. Should I leave? Coming here was a mistake. I did it so I could try to forget everything for a while, but it feels like I'm standing at that intersection again.

Those sirens . . .

I just stood there, like I was watching a movie and there was nothing I could do.

I should have gone to Mariposa, but I left her lying there in the street, all alone.

Then . . . a dull thud.

The car!

But Lexi calls my name—and I'm suddenly back in the here and now.

"Beau!"

The lid of the coffin has fallen onto the floor. Lexi gasps for breath.

There isn't actually someone inside the coffin, is there?

I try to look past Lexi—and yes, there is a body in the coffin. It must be a dummy. It must be. But still, I feel the hairs on my arms stand up.

Lexi hesitates for a moment, but then she leans forward and grabs something from the coffin.

"Please stay where you are," I hear her say to the corpse. "I just want to . . ."

When she turns back to me, she has a flashlight in her hand.

"What are we supposed to do with this?" She clicks it on and off a few times.

I look through the glass and see Zora, also holding a flashlight. They don't seem to have any idea what to do with it either.

Lexi walks over to the elevator and presses the button.

"No way it's going to be that easy," I say, repeating her words. "Maybe . . . maybe we should ask for a clue?"

I look at the ceiling. In the escape room I did before with Zora, there were cameras in plain sight, but there's no sign of any cameras here, just a few speakers for the robotic voice.

"There are no cameras," I say. I never imagined I might miss those things, but now a bad feeling is spreading throughout my body.

"Huh? How does that work?" Lexi frowns. "How's the gamemaster supposed to keep an eye on us?"

"Maybe there is no gamemaster."

"Don't be dumb. Of course there is. It's that Red. Isn't it?"

"Maybe the robot's voice is the only contact with outside."

"An escape room that's run by a robot?" Lexi laughs. "Are you out of your mind? The cameras are just high-tech ones, so we can't see them."

I look at the room next to ours. Zora is still standing there with the flashlight in her hand. She's studying it from every angle, as if there might be a secret code on it somewhere.

"Maybe we need to do something with the corpse."

I make the mistake of taking another look and then I really see who's lying there. The guy in the coffin—AJ, according to the ribbons on the wreaths—is not much older than me. He's wearing a button-down, a shiny watch, and a cap. His eyes are shut, but his eyelashes seem to be trembling, as if he might open his eyes at any moment. The dummy is so well-made that I can't tell it apart from a real corpse.

AJ reminds me of those figures in a wax museum. I went to one last year to unveil my own. They'd copied me so perfectly that it really creeped me out, standing there next to myself.

Fan selfies with my figure keep appearing online. Zora recently sent me one by a fan who'd undressed me. I'm standing there next to her in just my boxer shorts.

I hated it, but it made Zora totally crack up.

Lexi clicks the flashlight on and off a few more times. Then I realize something. The light isn't yellow or white, like with a normal flashlight, but purple.

"It's a black light. . . ." Slowly, it dawns on me. "Those things only work in the dark!"

Lexi looks at me. "How do you know that?"

I think about my new song. "We worked with a black light in my latest video."

"Your latest video?" Lexi sneers.

I have to bite my tongue. Zora would have shut her up straightaway, but I'm not in the mood.

"We need to turn off the lights," I continue. "And there's no switch, so we'll have to take out the bulbs." I try not to think about the fact that we'll soon be standing in the dark with three coffins.

"Go ahead, then." Lexi makes a gesture of invitation. "Climb up onto the coffins."

I'm about to say no way, but the look of challenge on her face convinces me.

I'm going to show this girl that I can do more than "pose like some wannabe model."

It's mean of her to pick on that anyway, because I've only ever done one modeling job. That underwear company paid so much that I couldn't say no to the deal. As if she'd turn down a job like that. . . .

"Fine by me." I pick up the lid from the floor and put

it back on the first coffin. I don't want to look at the wax dummy, but somehow death has a magnetic effect. Even though you don't want to look, your gaze is still drawn to it.

I can see that other coffin again, the one with the blue butterflies. I looked at that too. I had to do it. I forced myself to.

"How's it going?" I hear from behind me.

"Great!" The lid is finally back on the coffin. As soon as AJ is no longer visible, out of sight, it's easier to breathe.

I manage to hoist myself up onto the coffin. It's a bit wobbly. I don't even want to think about falling off and the dummy rolling out.

I carefully position my feet and find my balance. Zora and I went paddleboarding in the summer, and it feels just like standing on a board.

Carefully I stretch upward and, much to my relief, I can just reach the spotlight. Maybe my dad's tallness genes aren't actually such a bad thing.

I take out the bulb and the room becomes a little darker.

After the second bulb is out, half of Lexi's face is in shadow. I can barely make out her freckles. Soon it will be even darker.

It'll be just like when we entered the building. Only now I know what's inside the room.

At least one perfectly realistic dummy of a corpse.

Who's going to be in the next two coffins?

When I reach the last bulb, it gets trickier. The ceiling seems higher here. I have to stretch so far that it feels like my body is tearing.

I take out the last bulb. I can see that Zora and Tess have started to unscrew their bulbs too. The darkness returns.

It seems even blacker than before.

I instantly lose my balance. Any second now I'm going to fall off the coffin.

"The flashlight," I say.

There's no response.

"Lexi?"

Silence.

"Turn that flashlight on!"

LEXI

Truth be told, I hadn't expected Beau to climb onto the coffins.

"Lexi?"

His voice is almost pleading. Suddenly I get a glimpse of the *real* Beau, instead of the perfect version he pretends to be.

"Turn that flashlight on!"

I feel a smile on my lips.

Ladies first, but now it turns out this tough guy is scared of the dark.

I press the button. The flashlight fills the room with a strange purple light.

Beau glares at me. "What took you so long?"

I shrug. "It's on now, isn't it?"

Beau jumps off the coffin. "Give me that thing!"

He shines the flashlight on the brick wall. Some

symbols glow in the purple light. I look at the dots and dashes.

"Morse code," I say. "Why don't you try the same pattern with the light?"

Beau frowns. "What pattern?"

"You never played with Morse code when you were a kid?"

I remember a sleepover at Tess's. Kelly was there too, and each of us had a flashlight. We had entire conversations in Morse code. It was perfect. We didn't make a sound, so my aunt didn't realize we were still awake.

"Dots are short. Dashes are long." I take the flashlight and repeat the pattern on the wall. Nothing happens.

"Wait a second." Beau looks at me, above the purple glow. "Maybe we should do that with the elevator button!"

"Good idea!" I place the flashlight on the coffin and run to the elevator control panel. "Short, long, short, short, long." I take my finger off the button.

For a few seconds, nothing happens.

I'm about to turn and start searching the room again, but then I hear a loud *ping*. The elevator doors open.

I jump back. The elevator looks perfectly normal. But still, I get goose bumps all over my body.

The loud *ping* is echoing in my ears.

"Gentlemen first, then?" Beau steps into the elevator. Nothing happens, the doors stay open, and Beau looks at me expectantly.

"Are you scared it's going to go plunging down the shaft or something?"

"Of course not."

I look back at Tess and Zora, who are staring at our room. They're having trouble reaching their last light bulb to turn it off. I look at Tess. If I get into the elevator now, I'll be leaving her behind, but at the same time I want to beat her. I want to challenge her as much as I can, so that more and more of the old Tess will return. The Tess who will do whatever it takes to win.

If she's okay, so am I.

I carefully take a step forward. The elevator bounces very slightly under my weight, but then I'm standing in it, and Beau is looking at me from the side.

"Hey, you're still alive."

I point at the buttons. "Which floor?"

Then the robotic voice comes blasting into the elevator. *"Hello."*

I look at the elevator speaker, the kind of thing you'd hear security speaking through if you get stuck.

"You can choose. Do you want a clue for your next puzzle? Then press number four. If not, then go to floor two. But keep in mind: for every clue, someone will pay a price."

"A price?" I echo. "Like what?"

"They often add on extra time," says Beau. "They factor it into your score at the end. So what do we do? Are we going to make it without any clues?"

I look at the three coffins, which are still in the dark.

"I want to get out of here as fast as possible," I say. "I want to beat them."

"Are you really that competitive?" Beau looks at me in surprise.

"What do you mean?"

"Oh, you know. . . ." Beau smiles. "I didn't expect it from you."

"Why not?"

"Well, that phone of yours, your necklace, your . . ."

"What's wrong with my choker?" I reach up and touch the black plastic chain. Tess gave it to me when we were in elementary school, and I've never taken it off.

"What did you call it?"

"A choker," I repeat.

"It's old-fashioned," says Beau. "Zora had one like that years ago."

"So?"

"So it still works just fine, right?" Beau grins again.

I have to control the urge to punch him.

"Sorry, sorry," says Beau, holding up his hands and smiling. "You just don't look like you care that much about winning."

"Because I don't own any expensive stuff?" I raise one eyebrow.

"No, I just mean . . ." Beau changes the subject. "So we're going to get a clue?"

I nod.

"Cool." Beau presses the button with the 4 on it.

"You have chosen to receive a clue. That means someone will have to pay the price."

There's another loud *ping,* and the elevator doors slide toward each other. Just before they close completely, I catch a glimpse of the other room.

Tess's panic-filled eyes are looking at the ceiling.

And then I see what she's looking at.

Tess and Zora's room is filling with smoke.

CASE nr. 1999-5

E. Shepherd—psychiatrist

OBSERVATION:

The girl spins the pencil in her fingers but does not use it.

When I ask her what exactly she's waiting for, she asks me what the point of all this is.

I explain that it's sometimes easier to draw memories than it is to talk about them. That it could help her to process the experience.

This way, she can talk without having to use her voice.

She gives a deep sigh, but then focuses on the paper.

At first her movements are a little awkward, but then her pencil moves faster and faster across the sheet.

She draws for about five minutes.

<u>Scribbling on the paper, almost aggressively.</u>

Then she leans back and looks at me.

"This is what it was like in there" is all she says.

And then, with full force, she jabs the pencil into her own hand.

THIS
IS
WHERE
THE
GAME
BEGINS

BEAU

"Did you see that?" Lexi bangs on the elevator doors, but they stay closed. "What was that? Where did that smoke come from?"

"I . . . I don't know."

"Was it a fire?" Lexi's eyes grow wide. "That Red . . . She started a fire!"

"No, she didn't," I say, trying to reassure Lexi and myself. "No way."

"How do you know that?" Lexi bangs on the elevator doors again. "Did you see how scared Tess looked?"

"It was just one of those smoke machines, like they use at concerts."

Lexi blasts me with a glare. "You sure about that?"

"Y-yes." I can't help that my voice is trembling a bit.

"But where did that smoke suddenly come from? I mean . . ."

Then Lexi gasps, and she looks at me with wide eyes. "It's because of us!"

"What do you mean?"

" 'For every clue, someone will pay a price,' " Lexi says, repeating the words of the robot. "We caused this. And they're paying the price. They're in that fire because of us!"

"There is no fire!" I yell back at her, my voice cracking. "It's just a special effect to slow them down. There's no way they're going to let people die in here!"

For a moment, there's silence.

If Lexi doesn't cool it and shut up, I'm out of here. She can figure things out on her own. She needs to stop freaking out. I've already seen more than enough girls freaking out at my concerts.

"Chill. There is no fire. Seriously. They're just trying to mess with us. Escape Room 2.0, remember? Red warned us: this is no ordinary escape room."

"Yeah." Lexi finally lowers her fists.

At that moment, the elevator starts moving slowly. It sounds rusty, like it hasn't been used in years. Lexi stands silently beside me as I watch the numbers on the screen above the buttons change.

1, 2 . . . D . . . 3, 4 . . . E . . . A . . . D.

Dead?

I glance at Lexi, but luckily she hasn't seen it. I can't stand the thought of her pounding on the doors again.

This is just some kind of horror-themed escape room,

designed to scare the living daylights out of people. I've heard stories about them, but I never thought I'd go to one voluntarily.

But fair's fair: it's nicely done. I'm actually sweating for real. And just for a moment, I even forgot about LA.

The elevator jerks. There's a 6 on the screen now. How did that happen? We pressed 4, didn't we?

"Where are we going?" I whisper. The elevator stops with a jolt. Lexi has to hold on to the rail so she doesn't fall.

"What's going on?"

We wait for a few seconds, silently staring at the 6.

Nothing happens.

I lean forward and press the 4 button again, but the elevator stays put. I look at the screen, but nothing is happening. No letters, no numbers.

"What now?"

"We wait. I think."

"What for?" Lexi is running her finger over the buttons.

"Don't do that," I say, but I'm too late. Lexi presses the alarm button. And the light goes out.

"What do you think you're doing?" I check my pockets, then realize I left the flashlight on one of the coffins. Why didn't I bring it with me?

"Calm down. I'll just press it again," I hear Lexi say. At that moment, the elevator plummets. I feel my stomach flip. We drop yards in seconds.

And . . .

Back up again!

Lexi screams.

"Lexi!" My voice sounds like it belongs to someone else. The elevator has gone haywire. "What are you doing?!"

But all Lexi is doing is screaming.

The elevator drops again. It's like a roller coaster, and it's making me want to puke. Every time I think it's over, we go crashing back down. And then shooting up again. The red digits on the screen are flashing wildly.

Then I see letters again. I clutch the metal handrail and try to follow what they're spelling out.

1, 4, 6, 2 . . . I . . . 5, 2 . . . L.

Ill?

But then the sequence begins again. I missed a letter at the beginning: the *P*.

Pill?

Does this have something to do with the escape room? Or is it just some kind of error code?

I retch. We keep shooting up and down. Any minute now I'm going to throw up all over everything. . . .

But then the elevator finally comes to a stop. A red 2 appears on the screen. The rail feels wet under my sweaty hands, and I brace myself to go plummeting down again.

That doesn't happen.

Instead, the doors of the elevator slide open.

LEXI

I trip up over Beau and crash onto the floor beside him. As soon as we're out of the elevator, the doors slide shut again. It's so quiet.

My heart is pounding against the floor. I swallow the taste of vomit in my mouth.

What *was* that? It was like the elevator came to life. If only I could tell Tess not to set foot inside the elevator.

Tess . . .

I see her in front of me again, in that room full of smoke.

She looked so scared.

Beau's probably right about it being some kind of effect, but what if there really is a fire? Maybe the price our opponents are paying for our clue is a really high one.

No.

Don't even think about that.

But who says we can trust Red? None of us knows the

woman behind the telephone number. Beau and I both just went ahead and called the number and accepted her invitation.

And what's even worse is that I dragged Tess into it. I was trying to distract her, to pull her away from the Shadow for a while, but what if I put her in serious danger? I'll never forgive myself.

And Lonnie will never forgive me either. What's she going to say when she finds out what I've done? My aunt trusts me.

I found Tess by the highway that night.

It was me who held her tight in the hospital.

I was the one Tess told she was hearing voices.

I was the only one she still wanted to have around her.

Lonnie said I was a gift from heaven. But will she still think that when she hears about this escape room?

I have to go back to the first floor. I need to know if Tess is really okay.

Beau scrambles to his feet. I do the same.

We press the button by the elevator, but the doors don't open.

"Hello?" I shout. "We'd like to go back downstairs."

There's no reaction.

Red *is* here, isn't she?

A bad feeling spreads throughout my body. What if Beau's right and there is no gamemaster?

What if we really are at the mercy of that robotic voice? Then the only way out is through the puzzles.

No.

That can't be true.

Red just wants to scare us, like she did with that smoke.

I finally look around the space we're in. We're standing in a room that's lit up only by a small lamp and a neon advertisement for beer. There's a single bed and a desk, and on the walls are black-and-white photographs of a boy on a skateboard. He looks familiar. Then I see the graffiti on the wall behind the bed. The bright colors make up a name: AJ.

"Th-that boy in the coffin," I stammer. "This is his room."

"Hello. You've made it to a new room. Congratulations," says the robotic voice. *"Show respect as you search the room. Remember that you are guests in this place."*

Not a word about the other team, about whether they're okay.

That must mean everything is all right. Right? I need to stay calm. Tess didn't want a babysitter, so I won't be one. She can take care of herself. That's what she said before we came in here.

Beau runs his hands over the wallpaper. Isn't he bothered by any of this? He hasn't said a word about Zora yet.

"Aren't you worried?" I ask in surprise.

Beau looks at me. "What about?"

"About Zora!" I sigh. "Do you only ever think about yourself?"

Beau's eyes narrow, and he takes a step toward me. "You don't know anything about me."

His voice sounds even deeper than usual. I have to tilt my head back to look at him, because Beau must be more than a foot taller than me.

We stare at each other for a few seconds, but Beau is the one who gives up. He turns away from me.

"I'm going to search the room."

I'm about to tell him he's an arrogant jerk, but I bite it back.

I feel under the mattress, but there's nothing there. The comforter's not hiding any secrets either.

"Find anything?" I ask after a few minutes.

Beau doesn't reply.

"What do you think the gamemaster meant by *respect*?"

Beau shrugs.

"You going to stay silent?"

Beau looks at me. "Why should I say anything to you?"

"We're a team," I reply. "Whether you like it or not. You're just offended because I told you the truth. Did no one ever tell you that you only think about yourself?"

A muscle in Beau's temple is twitching. Give it a bit longer and I'll get him to explode. I know his weak spot.

I always find weak spots pretty fast. It's become a special talent of mine.

My aunt's weak spot is Tess's medication. Tess's weak spot is Kelly. And mine is Tess.

"Well, then, let me tell you: you are a horrible team player! You're probably used to everyone admiring you, with those lovely curls of yours, but not me. You're no use to me at all. You just stand there shrugging and making like everything's okay, and meanwhile—"

"You have no idea who I am, do you?" Beau interrupts me.

"What do you mean?"

"Never heard of . . . BEAU?" Beau says his name as if it's written in capital letters.

"Yeah, that's you, isn't it?"

Beau's eyebrows shoot up, and his jaw drops. "You really don't have a clue."

"What I do know is that you're a spoiled, arrogant, lazy—"

In the middle of my sentence, a big grin appears on Beau's face, and then he bursts out laughing.

BEAU

"What?" Lexi is getting even madder. "Why are you laughing?"

My stomach's shaking so much now that it's aching. Lexi doesn't recognize me. This girl has no idea who I am.

She's not a hater. It's just that she actually does hate *me*. Me personally.

And for some reason, that feels so good that I can't stop laughing.

Lexi's eyes blaze like her red hair. "What kind of idiot are you?"

But that just makes me laugh even more.

How long has it been?

These past few months, I haven't had much reason to laugh. It's like my body doesn't even recognize the movement anymore.

"You know what? Forget it!" Lexi turns around. "From now on, you're on your own."

"N-no." I hiccup. "It's n-not about y-you."

"What is it about, then?"

"About Beau!" My laughter slowly dies away until only my stomach is shaking a little bit. "You don't know Beau!"

"You're Beau," says Lexi. "And unfortunately I do know you."

"No, I mean 'BEAU,'" I say, doing air quotes. "The brand."

"The *what* now?"

I have to hold in another fit of laughter. Has she been living under a rock or something? Her cousin recognized me—I'm one hundred percent certain of that.

"I'm famous."

Lexi frowns. "Never heard of you."

"No," I say. "I noticed."

"So that's why you're laughing at me?"

"No, I'm not laughing at you." I try to look serious. "I just find it . . . liberating."

"Well, that's nice for you. So, where am I supposed to know you from?"

"I'm a singer. You never watch stuff on YouTube?"

Lexi shakes her head.

"How about the news?"

"Why would I? It's only ever bad news." Lexi sniffs. "If there's anything important, I hear about it from Tess or my mom and dad." She looks at me. "Seems you weren't important enough."

I know she's trying to insult me, but it doesn't feel like that anymore. It's actually like the room is less claustrophobic.

"You going to stop laughing, then?"

I make a show of wiping the smile off my face. "Promise."

"Fine. We don't have any clues. So what do we do now?"

"Wait a moment." I point at the elevator. "There was a clue!"

I remember the changing digits in the elevator, alternating with letters. Could they have meant something after all?

"There was something in the elevator," I say. "Some letters appeared on the display, as well as the numbers. There was a word . . . It was *dead*. And then there was another one. . . ." I rack my brain. What was it again?

"*Pill!*" I yell. "It was *pill!*"

"Huh?" Lexi looks at me. "So why didn't I see it?"

"You were too busy screaming."

Lexi makes a face, and I quickly continue.

"*Dead* and *pill*," I repeat. "Do you think this AJ guy overdosed?"

At that moment the beer ad on the wall flashes.

"Did you see that?" Lexi's eyes grow wide. She runs over to the light and says, "AJ overdosed."

The light flashes again.

Lexi leans over a lamp and I hear a cracking sound.

"What are you doing?" I ask.

"Check this out." Lexi takes the shade off the lamp and puts it on the floor. The small fluorescent tube inside has four digits on it. They were hidden inside the light like a message in a bottle.

"It's a code." I go over to stand beside her, my blood racing through my body. There's something addictive about this escape room. I suddenly have tons of energy. Or maybe it's because I finally had a good laugh again for the first time in ages.

"It must be for something in this room." Lexi looks around. "We've missed a combination lock somewhere."

"Maybe under the rug?" I lift it, but all I see is wooden flooring. "Behind the photographs?" I take the photograph of the skate park off the wall, but all I see underneath is wallpaper.

"There, maybe?" Lexi points to the portrait of AJ.

He's looking past the camera, as if he felt embarrassed when the photo was taken. How did they actually get these portraits, anyway? What kind of model would allow themselves to be used for an escape room like this one? I'd hate to think of an escape room using me as a dead person.

As soon as Lexi takes the photograph off the wall, the screaming starts.

"Get your hands off me!"

For a moment, I think it's the robotic voice again, but this sounds different. And then I realize that the voice is coming from the photo.

The portrait of AJ is moving.

Lexi shrieks. She lets go of the photo and together we look at the boy, who's staring at us furiously. It must be some kind of digital trick, but it really does seem as if the photo has come to life.

"Look, I know I shouldn't have stolen those pink pills from my friends. But I'd had enough. It's so fucking black here. I'm sorry, okay? But what's the point? I'm not coming back, never again!"

Then, as suddenly as AJ came to life, he falls silent. It seems like a perfectly normal photo now, just like the pictures next to it.

The silence lasts for a few seconds. Lexi is the first to speak.

"What *was* that?" She looks as pale as AJ's body down-stairs.

"That was AJ," I say, gasping. "Did you . . . did you see there's something behind the photo?"

"*Behind* the photo?" echoes Lexi. "All I saw was that guy. Did you see how real he looked?"

"I think there's a safe behind the frame," I say. "Give me a second."

I take a step forward.

"Not again." Lexi holds me back. "Please, no!"

"I think I . . ." I try not to look at AJ's dark eyes as I carefully take hold of the edges of the frame.

"Sorry, AJ," I say quietly. My hands are shaking, but I'm almost certain that I shouldn't tilt the photo.

It's like that old game, the one where you have to move a metal hook around a track without touching a wire. If you do touch it, it buzzes, and you're out. Zora always used to be amazing at it, but my hands would never cooperate. Whenever I get nervous, my hands tremble like crazy. You can even see it happening in some of the fans' videos. It's a miracle that I never drop my microphone.

Lexi watches as I gently lay the photograph on the floor. "How . . . ?"

"With *respect*," I say breathlessly. "That was the gamemaster's clue, right?"

A look flashes across Lexi's face. I can't quite describe it, but it's like her freckles start to glow for a moment.

Then I see the safe in the wall. It's a square metal thing, like I've seen in movies. There's a dial on the front with lines and numbers on it.

"The code in the beer light," I say. "What was it?"

Lexi glances over her shoulder. "One-nine-six-six."

I turn the wheel and hear a few clicks. Is the code right? Then there's a *clunk*. It worked!

I pull the door open and peer into the safe. I'd been

imagining all kinds of things, but not this. Inside the safe, there's a huge metal ring with loads of different key chains attached.

"Give it here?" Lexi studies the brightly colored labels. "They have numbers on them. What are we supposed to do with them?"

Behind us, we hear the familiar *ping*. The elevator doors slide open again.

Lexi is startled, looking at the elevator and then at me.

Is she thinking the same as me?

There's no way in the world I want to go back into the elevator, but I know we have to. We need to keep going, and that elevator is the only way out.

"Okay," I croak. "We're not going to buy any more clues."

"No," Lexi says quietly.

We walk to the elevator, and I look at her.

"Together?"

Lexi nods. "Three, two, one."

At the same time, we each put one foot in the elevator. Nothing happens. Then we each add our other foot.

The elevator gives a little wobble. I hold my breath.

The doors slide shut.

"Hello. Please select your floor."

Without asking me, Lexi presses the 1. She wants to get back to Tess as quickly as possible.

I think about Zora. Lexi's comment hit home, because

she kind of had a point. I'm not worried about my best friend. At least, not *really*.

Not because I don't care about her, but because Zora is Zora.

She's like a rock. She's never uncertain or scared. When she stood up for me against those kids at school, she took on three of them at once.

She's the one who yells at my fans to step back a bit at my meet-and-greets. She makes sure I get to the car safely, without them coming too close. She's actually like a kind of bodyguard.

But if that smoke was real, then Zora's in danger.

I'm the worst best friend ever.

As the elevator starts moving, I tense all my muscles. Luckily, it's going at a normal speed this time. I count the seconds, staring at the red digits. There are no letters this time. The 2 changes to 1 and then the doors slide open.

I jump out and I'm back in the room with the coffins. I never imagined I'd be so happy to see those things again.

But Lexi and I immediately notice a change: Zora and Tess's room is empty now. The smoke is gone, but so are the two of them.

How is that possible? Where did they go? How did they escape without removing all the bulbs?

"Tess?" shouts Lexi. "Where are you guys?"

I walk to the glass and place my hand on it. Then I look

around the room, as if Zora might be hiding behind one of the coffins.

But Zora is nowhere to be seen. My best friend is gone.

Then I spot something else. For a moment, I think I must be mistaken, but then my heart skips a beat.

Pulling my sleeve over my hand, I rub frantically at the glass. Lexi can't see this or complete panic will break out.

Come on, I think. *Please. Just go away.*

But there's absolutely no point.

The blood is on the other side.

LEXI

Beau is wiping away at the glass with his sleeve.

"What are you doing?"

He looks up, like he's been stung by a wasp. "Nothing."

"What *is* that?" I look at the glass and see a smear of red. "Is it . . . ?"

"Calm down," says Beau. "It . . . it's only a little bit of blood. If they were seriously wounded, there would be much more."

But I can't hear him anymore. I feel like I'm back inside that elevator, plummeting.

"Tess!" I bang on the glass, even though I know it won't help. No matter how hard I thump, no one is going to hear me.

"They got into the elevator. They're probably having the same shitty ride now as we did." Beau points at the wall behind us. "Maybe they saw our code. The robot said we might be able to copy from each other, didn't it?"

I rub my hand over the smear of blood and peer at the floor. There's no sign of any drops of blood.

"They probably banged too hard on the glass," says Beau. "Panicking because of the smoke."

"The smoke we sent their way!" My voice cracks. How could we have been so dumb? We never should have pressed that button!

I walk to the exit and try the handle. It doesn't budge.

"This is not an exit," says the voice.

"We want out!" I yell. "Can anyone hear us? We're done. We quit."

Nothing happens.

"Hello? Let us out!"

No reaction.

Panic creeps into my body like the smoke in Tess's room.

"How long have we been in here?"

Beau rolls up his sleeve and looks at his watch.

"Nearly two hours."

"Two hours?!" I feel the blood drain from my face. "Normal escape rooms usually take an hour, don't they?"

Beau doesn't say anything else. I want him to disagree, to tell me to stay calm, but he doesn't.

Slowly it dawns on me. There is no gamemaster, there are no cameras, no hints, and there's no emergency button.

We're not getting out of here.

We dropped our cell phones into the lockbox. We let ourselves be herded into this place like sheep.

I look again at the smear of blood. Whose blood is it? Zora's or Tess's?

In a couple of hours, Tess has to take her medication again. What's going to happen if she doesn't have it in time?

You will keep an eye on Tess, won't you?

"We have to get out of here, Beau." I walk to the first coffin and slide the lid off again.

"What are you doing?"

"I'm going to ram the door." I'm trying with all my might not to look at AJ. Since we were in his room and heard his voice, it feels almost like he really existed.

The lid of the coffin is so heavy I can barely hold it. As fast as I can, I bash it into the door, but the back end drags across the floor, so it feels like no more than a pat on the back.

"This is not an exit," says the robotic voice again.

"Lexi?"

I slam the lid against the door for a second time, harder now.

"This is not an exit."

"Lexi!" Beau grabs me by the arm.

I shake him off. "Get off!"

"I'm worried about Zora too," says Beau. "But there's

no point in panicking. That's not going to help your cousin. We have to stay calm."

"I don't have the time to stay calm."

"Why not?"

I take a deep breath. "She's sick, okay?"

Silence.

"Tess? She's sick? What's wrong with her?" Beau asks after a moment.

"She's on medication. And if she doesn't take her pills on time, the Shadow will come back."

I drop the lid. The dull thud sounds as if I'm giving up.

"The Shadow?" Beau echoes.

"That's what Tess calls her dark moments. She says it feels like there's a shadow following her all the time, and sometimes it catches up with her and enters her body. When that happens, she's . . ."

Crazy, I'm about to say, but bite my tongue. That's not right.

"Not herself?" says Beau, finishing my sentence for me.

I nod. "Something like that."

"That sucks," says Beau quietly. "What happens when . . . when the Shadow is inside her?"

"She sees things that aren't there." My eyes dart to AJ in the coffin. "Scary stuff. Like spiders running across the floor. Or she hears voices."

I remember that night when we were watching TV

and Tess screamed and pulled her legs up onto the sofa. I laughed at first because I thought it was because of the movie.

But that night Lonnie heard the front door slam. Tess had left the house and was missing for hours. When I found her by the highway, she said that a woman's voice in her bedroom had told her to get out.

Lonnie took Tess straight to a doctor, who prescribed medication for her.

"She can do dangerous things," I say.

Beau glances at the smear of blood, his face turning white.

"Zora . . ."

"No," I say quickly. "Tess wouldn't do anything like that."

"How can you be so sure?"

I think about Tess in the car with Lonnie the other day. She hadn't taken her pills. Lonnie told me that halfway through the drive to the forest, Tess suddenly grabbed the steering wheel. Lonnie had to fight to keep the car on the road.

Maybe Beau's right and I can't make any promises.

"Come on." Beau finally grabs the back half of the lid. "We have to get out of here. Three, two, one."

As hard as we can, we slam the lid into the door. We ignore the voice telling us that this is not an exit, and we pound the door, over and over again.

For Tess, I think with every thud, but it's pointless. It's like trying to break through a concrete wall.

With a yell, I drop the lid.

"What do you want from us?!" I bang my fist against the metal. "Let us out!"

Beau comes and stands beside me. For a moment I think he's going to try to stop me, but then he joins in. We both scream like our lives depend on it. We bang on the door, punching it and kicking it.

"This is not an . . . This is not an . . . This is not an ex . . . This is not an exit."

I don't stop until my knuckles are red and my voice is hoarse.

Beau looks at me, panting. "Well, that didn't work. But it did make me feel a bit better."

I look back at the door. There's a very small dent in it, like that time my dad bumped into a post when he was parking.

"You were screaming louder than AJ." Beau shakes his head. "If this place weren't in the middle of nowhere, someone would definitely have heard you."

I gasp and look at him. "That's it!"

"What?"

"AJ . . ." The gears inside my head are spinning at full speed. I try to remember what he screamed, because I'm sure every word counts.

"What AJ said!" I grab the bunch of key chains we found in the safe. The dozens of colored labels rattle against each other.

"He said something about pink pills, didn't he? And"—I take the only pink key chain, the one with the number seven on it—"what other color did he mention?"

It's silent for a moment, but then Beau picks out the black one, number eleven.

"He said it was black, didn't he?"

For a moment, our hands touch. His skin is dry and warm.

I felt that.

"Seven-one-one," I say quickly. "That must be the code for the second coffin!"

A few steps and we're beside the white painted coffin. When I key in the code, the lock springs open.

The adrenaline comes flooding back. There is an exit. The voice said so. At the end of the escape room, we can leave.

We have to solve the puzzles. That's all that counts. When we're out, we can fetch help.

The smoke was bad, but our best friends escaped from it. We have a chance of getting out of here in one piece.

"Shall I?" I look at Beau across the top of the coffin.

"Go for it."

I think he'd really just prefer to run away, but this time

I don't even think about making fun of him. AJ's room changed something. This escape room could scare anyone to death. Literally.

Who's it going to be this time? A woman? An old man?

I slide the lid to one side and the second face appears. I can hear Beau gasping, and my own breath catches in my throat.

Inside the purple-lined coffin, there's a girl. She has a chain with a locket around her neck. And on that locket a name is engraved—a name I don't have to read.

"I—I—I know her," I stutter. It feels like someone just punched me in the gut. "That's Kelly."

CASE nr. 1999-5

E. Shepherd—psychiatrist

AUDIO RECORDING:

"How did you sleep?"

"How would *you* sleep in this place?"

"Are you afraid to sleep?"

[. . .]

"We often use our dreams to process things we didn't deal with during the daytime. So it makes complete sense that all kinds of things come up at night."

"I want to go home."

"We've talked about that. It's not an option yet. As long as you're a danger to yourself, you're staying

here. Are you sure you wouldn't like
a sleeping pill, to help you calm
down a little?"

"No. I need to stay alert."

"It would do you good to relax for
a while."

[. . .]

"Don't you think?"

"The last time I let down my guard
for a moment, I got locked up for
hours. So no thank you."

THIS
IS
WHEN
IT
GOES
NEXT-
LEVEL

BEAU

Lexi steps back. And again and again, until she's standing with her back against the brick wall.

"Make it go away. Make her go away." Lexi claps her hand over her mouth and gags. "Close that lid!"

I push the wood, but too hard, and the lid goes clattering to the floor on the other side.

"Away!"

"Yes!" Now I'm screaming too. "I'm doing my best, okay?"

This time it works. The lid covers the girl.

Did Lexi really say she *knew* her?

Lexi still has her hand over her mouth. Her hair is hanging wildly around her face.

"Who . . . ?" I begin carefully. "Who is it?"

"Kelly," says Lexi again. "It's Kelly. Kelly. That's impossible, isn't it? What . . . what's she doing *here*?"

Lexi is so pale that I'm worried she's about to faint.

"Who's Kelly?"

"Tess's neighbor." Lexi gulps behind her hand. "She . . . she died from suicide in September."

I feel my stomach flip.

September.

Mariposa.

And suicide? Just like AJ!

I look at the first coffin. AJ is a work of fiction. His room and those photos of him are fake.

Aren't they?

What if he really existed, just like this girl did?

I stand up and put the lid back on AJ's coffin too. I don't want to look at him for a second longer.

"Don't you recognize her?" Lexi lowers her hand. Her lips are white. "Kelly's photo was all over social media."

I see the white coffin with the butterflies on it again. I haven't looked at any news sites since then, let alone checked out social media. I did just the same as Lexi always does.

"I don't know her. Sorry."

"How could they do this?" Lexi shakes her head. "Kelly really existed!"

I look again at AJ's coffin. An escape room with *real* dead bodies. Is that what Red meant when she said this was no ordinary escape room? This is going way too far!

"Kelly got bullied," Lexi continues. "And Tess feels guilty. She thinks she didn't do enough to help her."

Again, I see Red's face in front of me. A thought flashes past, so quickly that I can barely keep up with it. It's like graffiti in a tunnel when a subway train races through before you've had the chance to take a good look out the window.

"What . . . what if that's why Red chose us?"

"Us?" Lexi turns even more pale.

"As revenge for Kelly's death?"

"But there was nothing we could do about that!"

"I know that," I say quickly. "But maybe Red doesn't."

"You could be right." Lexi turns even paler. "Perhaps we *are* here for a reason."

I look at the third and final coffin. What if there's a little girl with curls in there? An eleven-year-old?

Mariposa.

"Red must hate us," whispers Lexi. "But why? I've never seen the woman before. I'm absolutely certain of that."

"What about Tess?" I ask. "Do you think Tess knows her?"

"She never met her," says Lexi. "I was alone when Red gave me that card."

"Zora didn't see her either."

I think back to Thursday night. What if I'd just thrown away the business card instead?

No one forced us to come. All four of us are here of our own free will.

I slide down the wall and Lexi does the same.

"Does anyone know where you were going?" she asks. "Or didn't you tell anyone either?"

"No. My manager thinks I'm staying in bed all day."

"So nobody knows we're here?" Lexi sighs. "Great."

"Hang on." I think about the deserted road on the way here. "Those guys . . ."

Lexi looks up. "Which guys?"

"When we were on the way here, a car with five guys in it started driving beside us. The one in the passenger seat took a selfie with me and asked where we were going. I told him the name of the escape room and the name of the street!"

"So?"

"If I don't come home this evening, my mom and dad are going to sound the alarm."

"Mine too," says Lexi. "But do you really think the whole country is immediately going to start looking for me?"

"They will for me."

Lexi raises her eyebrows.

"I mean it'll go straight onto my socials. Let's just say I've got a pretty big platform. So if that guy I met on the way here sees the post . . ."

"He'll know you're here?"

"Exactly." I breathe a sigh of relief. There's a way out. All we have to do is hang on until they come for us.

"Then let's hope you're as famous as you think you are," says Lexi. "And that the guy actually remembers you."

"His girlfriend's apparently *totally in love* with me," I say. "So I think he will."

Lexi sighs. "You really are the worst, you know that?"

I look at her. "Huh?"

"Every time I think you're actually kind of okay, you come out with something like that!"

"But it's true!" I say, defending myself. "He said so himself."

"You are *so* arrogant."

"I am not!"

"Yeah, you are." Lexi crosses her arms. "You don't even see it yourself anymore."

"If I'd gotten bigheaded, Zora would have told me," I say. "Believe me."

"Maybe she's just another of your fans too."

I'm about to open my mouth to reply, but I can't. I haven't told Zora anything about LA. Why not? Because I know she'd completely flip. And she would definitely want to come with me.

"We have to keep going with Kelly," I say. When I say her name, Lexi flinches. I don't want to hurt her, but I don't want to talk about Zora anymore either.

"We have to open it again." I jump to my feet and walk to the middle coffin.

"No way. Don't do that," hisses Lexi. "Do you know how disgusting . . ."

At that moment, we hear three loud thumps.

Lexi yells at me. "What are you *doing*?!"

"Me?"

"You just knocked on that coffin! It's not funny."

"I didn't do anything."

Another three thumps.

"You . . ." Lexi shoots to her feet.

"It wasn't me!" I hold up my hands. "Seriously!"

Two more dull thuds, and then it's silent.

"What . . ." Lexi's voice catches in her throat. "So . . . where did that knocking come from?"

I look at Kelly's coffin, which is still closed. I don't want to say it, but the words come rolling out.

"It came from inside there."

LEXI

What kind of sick joke is this? I look at Beau, but his hands are still in the air. It wasn't him, so it must have been Kelly.

For a moment, I think maybe she's alive, but that thought is so dumb that I instantly dismiss it.

Kelly is dead.

Has been for months.

The girl inside this coffin is a look-alike. A sick Barbie doll.

"It must be some kind of trick," says Beau.

I can feel my blood boiling. How dare someone use Kelly for this escape room?

Red has no idea what it was like when Kelly died. Tess wanted to read every article about Kelly. Every day she brought up some new piece she'd found online.

Those articles were like lashes from a whip—she used them to torture herself.

I look at the room beside ours. What if Tess manages to open that middle coffin and sees Kelly lying inside?

Then the Shadow will come rushing back—medication or no.

Medication.

How much time do we have? I look at Beau.

"Okay, we need to open the coffin." I try not to think about the waxy face inside. I deliberately didn't look into the casket at the funeral. I'd never seen a dead person before and I wanted to keep it that way. I was way too scared of having nightmares.

Tess did look. She didn't say anything when she came back. I just held her hand.

Lonnie said Kelly looked beautiful, but I didn't believe her. A dead person can't be beautiful.

"Okay, here we go." Beau slides the lid to one side, and I automatically look away. Any minute now, I'm going to throw up.

"I'll do the search," says Beau.

"Thanks," I say quietly, and then I hear him rummaging around.

How did Kelly end up in this escape room? Why would Red do something like this? Did she really choose us deliberately? But she only approached Beau and me. So it would seem that this is about *us*, not about Zora and Tess.

Unless she knew we'd choose them as our best friends.

"Wait a moment," says Beau. "I think I've found something. There's something in her locket."

How did Red manage to make her so lifelike? I think about the locket Kelly wore every day.

How did Red even know about that?

Because of the news, of course. The whole country was bombarded with pictures of her face.

Her death was big news for days. Tess even got pop-up notifications on her phone, like she hadn't already heard what had happened.

"It's a note." Beau clears his throat. "Do you . . . do you want to hear what it says?"

No.

No way.

"Go on, then."

" 'My worst enemies were disguised as my best friends, but if you'd like to speak to yours, you know where to find them. Press three times long and three times short on the bell. But beware: you'll need to talk fast.' "

Best friends who were actually her worst enemies. Red had clearly swallowed the news stories. Those girls weren't Kelly's friends at all. They were just plain old bullies.

But one article triggered another, and suddenly everyone was talking about a clique of friends. And that story sold well, of course.

Bullied by your own friends.

It was like Kelly's death was entertainment!

"So we need to press the bell," says Beau. "But it's on the outside of the building, isn't it? Then how are we supposed to . . . ?"

"The elevator," I whisper, turning to look at him. "The bell inside the elevator."

As if I've just spoken a secret code, the elevator doors suddenly open.

The note inside the locket was clear. If we want to talk to our friends, we can call them.

That means I can speak to Tess!

I dive into the elevator and look at the buttons. The bright yellow bell stands out from all the rest. The last time I pressed it, everything went crazy, but this time I know what the code is.

"Three times long," I say, repeating the words from inside the locket.

"And three times short." Beau has come to stand beside me and is holding firmly onto the rail. "We sure about this?"

"I've got to give it a try," I reply.

The elevator doors slide shut and we're locked up again inside the metal box, which feels like a two-person coffin.

I press the button. Three times long, three times short. My head is pounding. What if this is a trap and the elevator goes wild again?

But then there's a long note, like a telephone ringing.

I instinctively grasp Beau's hand, and he squeezes back.

We go on holding hands as the sound continues.

Am I *really* going to get to talk to Tess soon? In my mind, I picture her somewhere inside this building. Will she answer the phone in time?

And what should I say to her?

I at least need to know where she is. And if she's okay. I'll promise her I'll get her out of here, tell her she doesn't need to be afraid.

And I'll tell her not to touch the middle coffin too.

What's taking so long?

But then someone answers.

"Beau?" The agitated voice on the other end of the line is Zora's.

"Zora!" Beau dives for the speaker. "It's me!"

"That smoke!" yells Zora. "Why did you guys do that?"

"It wasn't deliberate. We—"

"Where's Tess?" I shout over Beau.

There's no answer.

"Zora!" I put my mouth so close to the speaker that my lips touch the metal. "Is Tess okay? Please, let her talk to me for a moment."

"That's not possible." Zora's voice sounds hoarse.

Something's really wrong.

"What do you mean, it's not possible?" I scream. "Just put her on the phone!"

"It's not possible," Zora repeats. "I . . . I don't know where she is."

And then the line goes dead.

"Zora!" I key in the code on the yellow bell again, but there's no point: Zora is gone.

"What did she mean? Why doesn't she know where Tess is?"

Beau is staring at his sneakers, as if the answer is written on them.

I can still hear Zora's voice echoing in the elevator. We don't know anything. We don't know where they are, or if one of them is injured, or . . .

All we know is that Tess isn't with her now. How did that happen? Did they get separated during one of the puzzles?

The thought of Tess all alone somewhere inside this building is freaking me out. This is a complete nightmare, even with Beau here. I can't imagine having to do it by myself.

"We're going to look for them." Beau finally looks at me. "And we're going to find them."

He sounds so confident that I feel a surge of hope go through my body.

"Hello." The robotic voice is back. "Which floor?"

That voice . . . All I really want to do is smash the

speaker to pieces with the coffin lid, but Beau points at a button.

"We still haven't been to the third floor. How about it?"

I feel like it doesn't matter where we go as long as we don't press the number 4. I can't bear the thought of anything bad happening to Zora and Tess again.

As soon as Beau presses the button, the elevator starts moving. I see the red digits on the display changing. I stare at them until my eyes start to water. Maybe there'll be another clue. I have to keep paying attention.

I see a 1, and then . . .

The elevator judders.

"No!" I grab hold of the rail. The elevator comes to a sudden stop. I count the seconds and say a quick prayer, even though I'm not religious.

"Come on," I murmur.

"Start moving," I hear Beau say.

But the elevator isn't listening. It stays put, as if it never worked at all.

"The other team has bought a clue."

I look up. "What?"

"That means you will pay the price."

"No . . ." Beau stares at the speaker. "Why would they do that? We told them the smoke was an accident!"

"Tess didn't hear that. Maybe she's panicking. . . ." I see Tess again in my mind's eye, all on her own somewhere. Of course she bought a clue. She wants to get out of here as fast as possible, and the puzzles aren't easy.

"What now?" Beau looks around, as if the elevator might have a secret door.

"Now we wait." I grip the rail tighter. What price are we going to have to pay? Is the elevator going to fill with smoke too?

"I hate small spaces," says Beau.

"Who doesn't?" I look at the display, on which I can now see a small red letter E, probably for *Error*.

"No, I *really* hate them."

When I look at Beau, I see beads of sweat on his top lip. His breath is coming faster and faster.

"Just calm down."

"Yeah, like that's an option." Beau looks around anxiously again.

"You have claustrophobia?"

"Yeah."

"What causes it?"

"Fans," he manages to gasp. This time he sounds anything but arrogant.

"How do you mean?"

"They . . . sometimes they . . . surround me." Beau sinks down the wall of the elevator and onto the floor. It's as if I'm not looking at *him* anymore, but at someone else entirely. He reminds me of Tess, the way he's sitting there with those big, frightened eyes. That was what Tess looked like when I found her that night by the highway. As if she'd taken drugs.

I do the same now as I did back then. I talk Beau through it.

"What exactly do these fans do?"

"There was this meet-and-greet once." Beau's voice is trembling, as if he's back there in that place. "Benji misjudged it. There were way more people than he'd expected."

"And what happened?"

"They swallowed me up. It . . . it was like being in the middle of the pit at the front of a rock concert. They were pushing me around, screaming and pulling at my shirt, flashing cameras in my face for pictures. . . ."

I try to imagine it. Beau surrounded by hundreds of out-of-control fans. It sounds terrifying.

"Then I fainted." Beau squeezes his eyes shut, as if he's in pain. "Some of the girls took photos of it."

"What a bunch of idiots," I blurt. "Who'd do something like that?"

Beau's eyes open. A faint smile appears on his pale face.

"Well, seriously?" I say.

"They take photos of everything," says Beau. "One time, I threw up onstage and the whole front row filmed it. It has the most views of any of my videos."

"That's seriously messed up."

Beau's smile gets even wider. "You sound almost mad about it."

"I *am* mad." I look at him. "It's just so dumb."

"What do you care? I thought I was just an arrogant, lazy—"

"Singer," I say, completing the sentence for him. "That's right. But not even you deserve that."

"That's the nicest thing you've ever said to me."

"Oh." I suddenly don't know where to look. "I had to do something to stop you from hyperventilating, didn't I? No way I'm giving you mouth-to-mouth resuscitation."

Now Beau *really* bursts out laughing. Just for a moment it's like we've both forgotten where we are.

Then Beau's laughter turns into coughing. He sighs. "I'm so thirsty."

Me too. I imagine an ice-cold glass of soda. I wish I'd said yes when Tess offered me a drink at her place. But I haven't had anything to drink for hours now.

And who knows how long this is going to take.

"Why on earth did you decide to do an escape room when you have claustrophobia?"

Beau looks at me. "I thought it'd only take about an hour."

Then the elevator starts moving. Finally. I just hope the clue was worth it for Tess or Zora.

The E on the display changes to a 2, and I hear Beau

sigh with relief. Not much longer and we can finally get out of this elevator.

When the doors open, Beau is the first to jump out.

It takes a few seconds for my brain to grasp what I'm looking at. The third floor is an empty room.

My eyes dart to the corners, the ceiling, the floor, but there's nothing to see.

There's no glass wall here either.

What's this supposed to be?

"There's nothing here. We should go somewhere else." But before I can turn to leave, the elevator doors shut behind us.

"What *is* this room?" Beau walks around, looking up and down.

AJ's room was scarily personal, but this one is almost more terrifying. The bare walls make the room feel like a big solitary cell.

"There must be something we're supposed to find here," I say.

"This has to be the room that's connected to Kelly, doesn't it?"

When I hear her name, I wince, like I always do.

Beau sweeps the palm of his hand across the concrete walls, as if he's checking the plasterwork. "Maybe we should bring the black light from downstairs," he says.

I look at the fluorescent tube on the ceiling, which

must be about ten feet high. "How are we going to turn this light off? Not even you are tall enough for that."

Beau sweeps his hand over the wall again. Suddenly there's a creaking sound, as if the wall is sighing.

Beau leaps back. "What was that? Did you do that?"

"I didn't do anything," I say, but then the wall makes the same sound again.

"The other team has bought a clue."

"No . . . ," Beau says. "Not again!"

"That means you will pay the price."

I don't understand. Why have they done it twice in such a short span of time?

But then I realize that's not right. Zora and Tess aren't together anymore. They each bought a clue, independently of each other.

"The walls!" Beau turns to look at me. "The walls are closing in!"

For a moment I think it's his claustrophobia again, but then I see what he means. The walls of the room are slowly sliding toward us. All four of them at once, like a box that's shrinking and shrinking.

Like a coffin . . .

"Stop!" Beau yells, his voice cracking. "Stop!"

He bangs on the walls, but there's no response. The robotic voice remains as quiet as the grave.

I look at the gray concrete mass that's slowly closing in on us. Panic rushes through my body, making me freeze.

"Lexi!" Beau pulls me away from the wall behind me, which is already pushing against my arm. The two of us are now standing in the middle of the room, as if on a little island in the middle of an ocean of concrete.

"Please!" Beau is still screaming. "Red, we want to leave!"

I don't want to beg for help, certainly not from that woman, but I still join in with Beau anyway.

"Please. We haven't done anything wrong!"

The creaking of the walls continues. Just a little longer and we'll be crushed.

So this is what it feels like to die.

I don't see anything flashing before me.

It's not like by the railroad tracks, where my senses are always on high alert.

Nothing about me feels alert here. I just feel completely numb.

Is this what Tess means when she talks about the Shadow?

"Lexi!" Beau's voice comes from far away. "There has to be a code. What's the code?"

Why does he keep screaming like that? There's no point anymore. Doesn't he get that?

"Lexi!"

I think about Kelly, about the wooden coffin, about her face surrounded by purple velvet. Soon it'll be me lying there like that.

Will my mom and dad cry? And Tess? Or won't she get out of this escape room alive either?

Beau and I are standing very close together now. His body is pressing against mine. I can feel his heart pounding against his ribs.

"We give up. Okay? You've beaten us. I'm sorry . . . I'm sorry about Mariposa." Beau bangs on the walls again, but it just seems to make them close in faster. "I know you know about that. But it was an accident, okay? An accident!"

What's he talking about? Who's Mariposa?

He needs to stop screaming. Red's not going to show us any mercy. That's never going to happen.

The two of us are now standing in a space that's less than three square feet. Way smaller than the elevator.

"Help!" Beau's voice is no more than a squeak. One last thump.

Thumping . . .

Suddenly I see everything sharply again. Kelly's coffin, the banging on the lid. I thought it was Beau playing a joke on me, but it was coming from inside.

Three times. Silence. Three times. Silence. Twice.

I knock my hand on the wall with that same rhythm.

Three times.

Silence.

The wall behind me is pressing into my back. What does it feel like to be crushed?

Three times.

Silence.

Any moment now and . . .

Twice.

And the creaking suddenly stops.

"What . . . ," begins Beau.

"Shh."

I'm way too scared that the wall will change its mind. We listen breathlessly. In front of me I feel the warmth of Beau's body, while behind me the ice-cold concrete wall presses into my back.

Beau's heart is thumping against my shoulder, making me dizzy.

Has it *really* stopped?

The creaking doesn't start again, but I still don't dare to move. What if the walls decide to keep going? Just another few inches and we'll be crushed.

"Lexi?" Beau whispers quietly.

I slowly look up. His face is so close that I can see every detail. His dark lashes, the hole in his nose where he once must have had a piercing, and his lips, slightly parted.

"What . . . ," he begins again, but then swallows the rest of his sentence. We press our mouths together.

BEAU

Lexi is kissing me as if it's the last thing she'll ever do. She presses herself closer to me, her lips exploring mine.

And then, as suddenly as she began, she stops.

The walls are creaking again.

Lexi grabs my arm, but this time the walls are moving away from us, as if the tide is slowly going out.

"What was . . . ?" I say, but Lexi shakes her head.

"Not a word about this." With a rough swipe of her hand, she wipes her mouth. "And you can take that grin off your face."

I hadn't even realized I was smiling!

Lexi takes a step back, as if she's afraid we might kiss again.

I think back to a meet-and-greet. One of the fans suddenly leaned forward and put her lips on mine. Before Benji could intervene, her tongue was already in my mouth. She tasted sickly sweet, her lips sticky with lip balm.

I was so stunned that I didn't push her away at first. Benji literally had to pull her off me.

I glance at Lexi, who is walking backward with the wall. This kiss felt very different.

"So what now?" I hear Lexi say. The walls slide a little farther, and then there's a final click. It's such a wonderful sound that the last slivers of fear melt away.

The click is followed by another sound, coming from above. When I tilt my head back, I see a small hatch open in the ceiling. I hadn't even noticed it was there.

A projector descends into the room, and then an image appears on the concrete wall. It's a forest with tall pine trees swaying gently in the wind. For a moment, it's like I'm really standing outside. Just for that instant, I feel free.

But then there's a faint clattering.

What is that?

I look down and see another projection on the floor. We're standing on what looks like a railroad track.

When I look to the right, I see the tracks continue. In the distance, headlights are approaching.

The train . . .

I'm about to step aside, but the tracks are as wide as the space we're standing in. It's impossible to escape.

The train is coming closer and closer.

Is this how Kelly . . . ?

I turn to ask Lexi, but she's not there. She's sitting in a

corner of the room, pressing herself against the wall. Her arms are over her head like a shield, and she's trembling.

"Lexi?"

At that moment, the train arrives. There's the sound of a horn and I see a flash of the driver, his face twisted in fear.

I know it's fake, but it feels like all the air is knocked right out of my lungs. I stagger as the train passes through me.

I just stand there for a moment, even after the train is long gone.

The clattering stops, and silence descends like mist.

I head to the corner of the room and reach out my hand to Lexi but leave it hanging midway. Maybe she doesn't want me to comfort her.

"Are you okay?" I ask quietly. There's no reaction.

"Lexi?"

Still no answer.

What if she gives up?

I can see why she would. I mean, she *knew* Kelly!

But I need her. I'm never going to solve this escape room on my own.

Lexi is obviously way better at solving puzzles than I am. She even knew how to stop the walls! If she hadn't been there, I'm sure we'd both have been crushed.

Red would have just let us die in here.

I think about Zora, somewhere else in this building,

looking for a way out. She's so close, but she feels farther away than ever.

How did I ever think she'd be able to fend for herself? Even wannabe bodyguards can die.

And Red is not going to spare anyone—that much is clear.

Who is that woman? Why did she choose Lexi and me? What do we have in common?

We both know someone who died: Kelly and Mariposa. But with Kelly it was suicide, and with Mariposa it was an accident.

So it can't be that.

I look back at Lexi, who's still shaking.

"Lexi?" I kneel on the floor and place my hand on her shoulder. Whether she wants it or not, she needs someone to comfort her.

"I'm here," I say quietly.

As soon as the words leave my mouth, I could kick myself. What difference does it make if I'm here or not?

But strangely, Lexi looks up now, her eyes filled with tears.

"That's how Kelly died." Lexi's voice is just a whisper. "She jumped in front of a train."

I nod slowly. "I'm sorry."

"There's nothing you can do about it," says Lexi. "But there *is* something I can do."

"Huh?"

"The same thing as her."

I frown. "What do you mean?"

Lexi stares at the spot where the train disappeared. The pine trees are still rustling in the wind.

"This is *my* railroad track."

Her track? What's she talking about?

"That's why Red wanted me," Lexi continues.

"What are you talking about?"

Lexi looks at me, her eyes almost drowning in tears. "I stand on this track every Thursday night until the train comes."

LEXI

"What?" Beau stares at me in confusion. "Why would you do that?"

"Because . . ." I can't say the words. No one knows about this.

"Well?" Beau persists. "Why would you do something like that?"

His expectant look is making me anxious. It's like the walls are closing in on me again and I have no escape.

"Because I . . . Because I want to *feel*."

"Because you *what*?"

I was right. He doesn't understand. Of course not, it's too dumb for words. I know that too.

But when I stand there on Thursday nights, it makes perfect sense.

"It's about the Shadow," I say quietly.

"What do you mean?" asks Beau.

"Tess's Shadow could be hereditary." I pause. "With

Tess, it appeared out of nowhere. It started with an empty feeling. That's what I'm so afraid of, that emptiness. So I check every week to see if I have it too."

"And you do that by the railroad track?"

I nod. "I stand and wait for the train to come."

"To see if you want to jump or not?"

"Not to jump!"

I think of Kelly.

Suddenly I see what Red must have seen. Standing by the tracks every Thursday night has nothing to do with Kelly, but what if Red knew Kelly, and she wants to punish me for doing it? Because she thinks it's disrespectful?

Maybe Red thinks I was one of Kelly's so-called friends, the ones the news keeps going on about.

"It's not about dying," I say to Beau. "It's about whether I feel anything or not."

I think about the magical moment when I feel the vibration of the rails against the toes of my sneakers.

"It's gross. I know that too," I say when I see the look on Beau's face. "But I have to know. You see? Then at least I'll be forewarned."

I look at the projection on the walls. Red chose *my* track for a reason.

"And what about Kelly? Is that the connection?" Beau looks at me. "You both stood beside the—"

"I would never jump," I say again. "That's not what it's about."

Suddenly the images are gone, and the projector disappears back into the ceiling.

"You won't necessarily get it, though, will you?" says Beau. "This . . . Shadow, I mean."

"Our moms are twins. Tess and I are really similar."

"She has black hair, and yours is red."

"She dyed it," I say. "She's just as much of a redhead as I am."

Beau has no idea how identical Tess and I really are. When we were little kids, we often used to tell people we were twins, and they always believed us.

It's only since the Shadow that Tess has changed. And when she dyed her hair black, it was as if the Shadow had literally taken over.

"People are always expecting pop stars to go off the rails one day," says Beau. "They're sure they're going to get dozens of tattoos just because they're bored or that they'll start drinking and doing drugs. Or take someone different home with them every week."

Then he pauses.

"But it's not like that," he adds.

"I don't care what you do," I say. "Really."

Beau runs a hand through his hair. We weren't going to mention the kiss, but now it feels like we're talking about it silently.

I have no idea what got into me. Maybe I was just afraid I was going to die, or I was relieved because the danger was over. Maybe I wanted to celebrate life. How would I know?

"What I mean is: sometimes the statistics are against you." Beau smiles. "But statistics are there to be beaten."

"You're right. We have to escape," I say. "Even if the statistics are against us."

"That's exactly what I was about to say."

Beau stands up and pulls me to my feet. When I'm upright again, it feels like I've been sitting on the floor for hours. My legs are tingling.

The elevator doors slide open automatically, as if they know we're done here. I feel Beau's hesitation. What if Zora or Tess buys another clue and we get stuck in there again?

"Come on." I grab his hand. "Forget the statistics."

Beau glances at our entwined fingers.

"Don't get any ideas," I say.

"I wouldn't dare."

We step into the elevator together, and it sighs under our weight. As the doors close, Beau presses the button for the first floor. We only have one coffin left now: the very last one.

"Fourth floor."

"Huh?" I press the 1 again, but the elevator is already going up. "Why isn't it working?"

The fourth floor. The floor we chose for a clue, the floor that got Tess and Zora smoked out.

"We didn't buy a clue!" I yell. "Leave Tess alone!"

But the robotic voice doesn't respond. It doesn't say anything about clues; the elevator just takes us silently to the fourth floor, where the doors slide open.

Even before my eyes can get used to what I'm seeing, there's a cry and someone comes flying straight at us.

CASE nr. 1999-5

E. Shepherd—psychiatrist

REPORT: EMDR SESSION

"Do you understand what we're going to do today?"

"EMDR."

"And did I explain it okay?"

"I follow your finger with my eyes, and I have to think about my worst memory. Then it'll vanish, just like with a magic trick."

"You don't think this is going to work, do you?"

"It sounds way too easy."

"It isn't. EMDR can be really tough. But some good results have been reported."

"And I'm your guinea pig?"

"Don't worry. This isn't my first time."

"But it *is* one of your first times."

"Try to trust me."

[A deep sigh.]

"Fine. Let's get started."

"I want to ask you first to picture an image of the memory that causes you the most anxiety. Do you have something?"

"Yes."

"What do you see?"

"Do . . . I have to say it out loud?"

"Please."

"I'm on the ground. Kneeling. I'm tired. My hands are dirty and sticky. I can smell earth."

"How would you rate your anxiety when you think back to that moment? On a scale of zero to ten?"

"A nine."

"And where in your body do you feel it most strongly?"

[She touches her stomach.]

"Okay. Then I'd like to ask you to follow my finger with your eyes. Back and forth. Very good. Now go back to that moment. What do you see?"

[Silence.]

"I see my own blood."

"Good. Focus on that."

[Silence.]

"What comes to mind now?"

"Earth. There was earth on my hands too."

"Focus on that."

"There was no way out. I had no place to go."

"How do you feel now?"

"Like I'm going to die."

"Follow my finger. Back and forth."

"I can't breathe."

"Follow my finger."

[She slams her fist on the table.]

"No, I don't want to!"

"Just sit down. Be calm. Like I said, the first time can be really tough, but . . ."

"To hell with your finger! This isn't working!"

    "I know this is asking a lot of
you, but it's important that we—"
    [She flips her chair over, sits in
a corner of the room, and remains
silent.]

**THIS
IS
WHEN
DEATH
APPROACHES**

BEAU

"Zora!"

I scream her name into a tangle of hair, which tickles my face and sticks in my mouth.

"Beau." Zora hugs me so tight I can hardly breathe. "You're here."

Together we stumble out of the elevator. In all the years I've known her, we've never held each other like this.

"You okay?" Zora steps back to take a look at me. She runs her thumbs over my face, touching every inch. "How are you doing?"

"I'm okay," I say, but then I see the blood on her shirt. "Are you . . . Are you hurt?"

"A bit." Zora raises her hand. There are bright red marks on her knuckles. "I hit that glass so hard when the smoke started. At first it seemed like part of the game, but then it just kept on coming. I seriously thought we were going to suffocate."

She must have been so scared. I feel so guilty about the smoke that I don't know what to say to her.

"Where's Tess?"

Zora and I both look up. Lexi is as pale as a corpse.

"Tess is . . . ," begins Zora.

"Let's just sit down for a moment," I say. I finally take a look at the room we've ended up in. The fourth floor seems to be a sort of waiting room, with a couple of sofas and armchairs. There's even a coffee table with a stack of magazines on it. If I didn't know any better, I'd think we were in a dentist's waiting room.

To my surprise, there's no glass wall and no identical second room. There is a second elevator, though, on the other side of the room. Was this designed as a space for meeting the other team?

"Where is Tess?" Lexi repeats. She refuses to sit down.

Zora drops onto a chair. "Tess is gone. When that smoke started, we panicked. I called Tess's name, but I couldn't see her anymore. Luckily, I found the elevator, and it suddenly opened. Then I yelled her name again. It wasn't easy, because that smoke was everywhere, and it was filling my mouth. Before I knew what was happening, the doors closed. I got out on the second floor, and when the coughing finally more or less stopped, I tried to go back downstairs. But the elevator doors were closed. It wouldn't work. So I just had to wait. It was minutes before the doors finally opened, and when I got downstairs, that floor was empty."

"Empty? What do you mean?" Lexi's freckles are an orange mask across her pale white skin.

"Tess must have taken the elevator after me and then gotten out on a different floor."

"And you didn't go look for her?!"

"I couldn't," says Zora. "The elevator wasn't cooperating."

"You just abandoned her in that smoke." Lexi says, her voice trembling.

"No, that's not true. The elevator doors suddenly shut!" Zora looks at me for help.

"You know what the elevator's like," I say to Lexi. And it sounds like their elevator is weirder than ours. And they didn't even have to solve puzzles to get into it.

"So Tess has been all on her own somewhere in here? All this time?" Lexi says despondently.

If it were Zora, I'd react exactly the same way. This escape room is terrifying when you're with someone else, let alone by yourself.

"I'm sorry," Zora says quietly. "I really have no idea where she is."

"How far did you get?" I ask. "Did you see AJ and Kelly?"

Zora frowns. "Who?"

"The bodies in the coffins," I say.

"We only got the first coffin open," says Zora. "You saw that, didn't you?"

"Wh-what were you doing all that time on your own?" stammers Lexi.

"I spent the entire time sitting in that damn elevator!" Zora yells. "When I tried to go look for Tess, the stupid thing got stuck. I only escaped just now!"

I think about when *our* elevator got stuck. That was for maybe a few minutes. Did Zora have to go through that all this time?

"Then I heard your voices through the speaker. It was the first sign of life. I was so relieved, so happy."

"And what happened then?" Lexi insists. "After we were disconnected?"

"I . . ." Zora's voice almost breaks. "The voice said I had to make a choice. Go back to my teammate, or back to Beau."

"And you chose Beau," says Lexi.

"Of course I did!" Zora's voice is thick with tears. All these years, I've never seen her cry, but now her eyes are overflowing. "What would you have done?"

"And that elevator just brought you straight to the fourth floor?" Lexi asks doubtfully. "You didn't have to do anything in return?"

"The voice said something I didn't understand." Zora wipes her eyes, but they fill right back up with tears again.

"What?" yells Lexi. "What did it say?"

Zora looks at me again, and I nod gently at her.

"That someone was going to pay the highest price."

LEXI

"Tess." I look at Beau. "Tess has paid the highest price."

"Not necessarily," says Beau. "Maybe that was the moment when the walls started to close in on us. So we were the ones who paid the highest price."

I look at Zora, who is hiding her face in her hands. What I really want to do right now is drag her around the room by her hair. She left Tess to fend for herself and chose to go back to Beau. She *knew* we were still together, but Tess is all alone somewhere. All this time . . .

And what if Tess was on the second floor when Zora chose Beau? Maybe the walls of her room started closing in too. She had no way of knowing Kelly's code, because they didn't get the second coffin open.

What if the walls kept closing in, until there was no room for Tess?

Until she . . .

"We have to get out of here as fast as we can," I hear Beau say.

"How?" asks Zora. "I just don't get how this escape room works."

"Lexi and I have come a long way."

"Have you opened all the coffins yet?"

"Except for the last one. So we need to go back."

"What then?"

"When we get that one open, I guess there'll be a final clue." Beau places a hand on my arm. "What do you think, Lexi?"

I look at his fingers for a moment, which were entwined with mine just a few minutes ago.

"I don't know. . . ." The energy I felt before has disappeared. All I can think about is Tess, between those four walls.

Zora looks around. "Which of the two elevators should we take?"

"Ours," says Beau. "We'll go to our room, because we're much further along in the game. Come on."

Zora points at the panel of buttons beside the elevator. It's different than the ones on the other floors. I count ten buttons on this one.

"So how do we get back into the elevator?" Beau runs a hand through his curls. "There must be a code."

"I bet it's in here somewhere." Zora starts leafing

through magazines. Beau leans toward her, and I hear him mumbling things to her.

"How about this?"

"We could try it." Zora keeps keying different combinations into the panel, but the elevator doors remain closed.

I know I should be helping, but I can't bring myself to do anything. I just can't shake off that image of Tess between those concrete walls.

We're in here because of me. I accepted an anonymous invitation from some mysterious business card.

But why?

Because I wanted to see if I'd feel something?

Well, it worked. I'm just about ready to explode with fear.

I wish I could turn back time to Thursday night. Then I'd tear the business card into a hundred pieces and throw them off the overpass. No bloodred letters, no phone number . . .

Hang on . . .

"The phone number!"

Zora and Beau look at me.

"What?" says Beau.

"It's Red's phone number!" I look at the buttons beside the elevator. Three rows of three, with one solitary button below.

"It's a telephone keypad!"

Beau's eyes grow wide. "Wow, you're right."

Zora stares at me. "You're good at this."

I don't react. She abandoned Tess, and I'll never forgive her for that.

Beau looks around. "You think her business card is in here somewhere?"

"Yeah, probably," says Zora. "But I know it by heart."

"You serious?" Beau exclaims.

Zora nods. "Yeah, I keyed in the number. Remember?"

"That was three days ago!"

"And?" Zora hurries over to the elevator and starts pressing the buttons. "It was something with lots of twos. Zero, six, four, two, two, two . . ."

A second later, the doors slide open. I can hardly believe my eyes.

Zora looks over her shoulder. "Are you guys coming?"

The coffins are lying there peacefully, as if nothing out of the ordinary has happened.

There should have been four of us here, but we're missing the most important person.

I try not to think about Tess, but I can't stop picturing her. Terrified, pale as a ghost.

Her medication will have almost worn off by now. She is supposed to take it at about this time.

Has Lonnie realized yet that something's wrong? Maybe she already called Tess.

Tess's phone is probably buzzing nonstop inside the lockbox. Maybe Lonnie's already out looking for us, with Mom. And they're driving around town now, like headless chickens.

"A code with four digits," says Beau when he checks the padlock on the last coffin. "Any suggestions?"

"No." Zora looks at the other two coffins. "Who did you say was inside those ones?"

"AJ," says Beau, and then he looks across at me. "And Kelly."

"Kelly Kleefman," I say.

"Kelly Kleefman?" Zora frowns. "Why does that name sound so familiar?"

"Because you've probably heard it before." I look at the middle coffin. "She died by suicide in September."

"Was that the girl who jumped in front of the train? Huh? She's inside that casket?"

I nod and I feel my stomach flip again.

"But . . . she existed for real."

I nod again.

"Wasn't Kelly that girl who was bullied by her friends?"

"They weren't her friends," I say. "Tess was the only friend she had."

Zora's eyes grow wide. "Tess *knew* her?"

"Yes."

"Wow." Zora shakes her head and curses under her breath. "I'm sorry."

"We need to find that code," I say quickly, turning my back on her. I don't want to talk about Kelly anymore, and certainly not here.

But no matter how hard I look, the room remains just as empty. It feels like Beau and I have already searched every last inch. Where are we supposed to find another clue?

My eyes flash across the streak of blood on the glass. The blood is Zora's, not Tess's, but I can hardly bring myself to look at it.

Without our clue, the smoke would never have happened. Then Zora wouldn't have panicked and run into the elevator, and Tess wouldn't be all alone now.

So I'm just as much to blame for Tess's disappearance as Zora is.

My eyes slide along the glass wall, in search of a four-digit code, but then flash back again.

On the other side of the glass, there's a girl. She's sitting on the floor between the first two coffins with her arms wrapped around her knees.

With her back to us, she's rocking to and fro, as if she's swaying to a catchy tune.

It's Tess.

CASE nr. 1999-5

E. Shepherd—psychiatrist

NOTES:

Months after the EMDR session, she gets in touch.

I'm surprised because she has resisted all previous attempts to contact her.

She's been back home for some time now, so we meet at my office.

When she enters the room, I see she's lost weight. There are dark circles under her eyes, and her skin is gray.

She sits down in the leather armchair and says that she wants to tell her story.

"I'm going to tell it in one go. Don't interrupt me." Those are her exact words. "I don't want any further treatment. I just want to tell my story once for your records. Then I'm done."

BEAU

"Tess!" Lexi is screaming louder than my fans at a concert. Zora and I both look up at the same time. For a moment, I think Lexi is having a complete breakdown, but then I see what she's seeing.

Her cousin, on the floor, on the other side of the glass wall.

Lexi throws herself at the glass like Zora flew at me when she saw me again. She's thumping and banging with her fists, but it makes just as little impact as before. Tess can't hear her.

"She's here!" Lexi turns around. "She's alive!"

Zora and I go stand on either side of her and pound the glass along with her. Not even six fists are enough to get Tess's attention.

"The lid." Lexi looks at me, and I immediately know what she means.

"I'll help you." Together, we take the lid off the first

coffin. I have no time to count to three, because Lexi starts slamming it into the glass. It makes a dull thud, but it's apparently loud enough to hear on the other side. Tess's shoulders jerk, and she slowly turns around. Her face is streaked, and her eyes are surrounded by black circles. It must be her mascara, but for a moment it makes me think of the Shadow that Lexi talked about.

When Tess sees us, her whole expression changes. Her empty gaze fills with hope.

She stands up and puts one hand on the glass. Tears stream down her cheeks.

"Tess, we're coming to help you, okay? Hang in there for just a bit longer." Lexi puts her hand on the glass too. Their hands are exactly the same size.

"Look at me." Lexi's eyes bore into Tess's. "Are you injured?"

Tess stares blankly at her, but I can see the bloodstains on her shirt. Where has she been all this time? What was this "highest price" that she had to pay?

"We should have taken the other elevator." Lexi looks at me. "Then I'd be with her now!"

She runs back to the elevator and smashes the button. "Open up! I want to go back to the fourth floor. Then we can take the other elevator down to Tess!"

"There's no point," I say quietly. "The elevator decides when we can leave."

"Stay out of this!" Lexi's face is as fierce as it was at the beginning of the escape room. She runs back to the glass.

"I can't even *talk* to her! Tess, listen to me. I'm coming. Okay?"

Tess frowns. Zora and I used to play a game where we had to get a message across to each other by lipreading. It sounds easy enough, but it's a real challenge.

"Tess . . ." Lexi's lips are so close to the glass that it's fogging up.

"Let me try?" I gently push Lexi aside. She's about to lash out at me, but I speak first.

"I have an idea."

She lets me move her out of the way, and I breathe onto the glass too, next to the spot where Lexi just did it. The spot of condensation grows larger. Then I draw in it with my finger, in mirror image, so that Tess can read it: *u hurt?*

Tess nods. She pulls up her shirt and I see a big cut running down her rib cage, with blood coming from it.

Lexi breathes on the glass again and promises Tess: *be out soon.* I have no idea how she's going to manage that, but I'd probably have done the same. Tess looks like she's been living in the wilderness for weeks.

"The code." Zora gives me a nudge. "How about we do it together?"

I know what she really wants to say: *leave Lexi alone for a while with Tess.*

I tear my eyes away from the girl on the other side of the glass and nod.

When we're beside the coffin, Zora leans toward me.

"I don't know if we're going to get out of here, Beau."

"Yeah," I say quietly. "But we have to try."

"This escape room is impossible."

"Not impossible." I point at the two other coffins. "But it *is* extremely sick. I'm so sorry."

"What for?"

"For bringing you with me. Without me, you wouldn't be here now."

"Without you, there are so many things I'd never have done." Zora makes a face. "I'd never have had someone to sit next to during the break. I'd never have had a real friend."

I look at her.

"What?" Zora looks back. "You know all this, don't you?"

"Yeah, but . . ."

"But what?"

"What about the business?"

"What business?"

"*My* business. The music business."

"Well, sure, it's fascinating," Zora admits.

I think about what Lexi said. Maybe she's right and Zora really is a fan. But she's more than that, much more.

Maybe I should tell her about LA. But not now, not

here. *When we're out of this place,* I promise myself, *I'm going to tell her everything.*

Zora nudges me again. "You're not going to start crying, are you?"

"Not yet," I say.

"Emo kid. Come on. How about we escape?"

I nod and look down at the lock again. Four digits, but which ones? What if I just try something? How many combinations are there? Hundreds? Thousands?

I tug at the lid, but it's so tight. It won't budge.

"I'm going to murder that Red woman when we're out of here." Zora says, looking at me across the coffin. "With her stupid business card. Did she really think we'd want to do something like this?"

I think about Benji, about the recording studio, about the endless stream of people approaching me on the street. In here, just for a while, I was simply Beau, without all the capital letters. Lexi hadn't even heard of me. In fact, I got exactly what I wanted: an escape.

I instantly dismiss that thought. I don't want to be grateful to Red for anything.

"I think she's enjoying all this. That Red is a total psychopath." Zora bangs her fist on the coffin.

"She seemed so normal." I remember meeting her. "I thought she was a fan's mom or something."

"Serial killers often seem normal," says Zora. "You know that, don't you?"

Serial killers. The thought makes me nauseous.

"*This is no ordinary escape room.*" Zora tries to imitate Red's voice.

"Her voice had more of a rasp," I say.

"Who cares?" snorts Zora, but then she continues in a raspy voice: "Like this, you mean?"

"Wow . . . exactly like that! How do you do it?"

Before Zora can reply, the robotic voice suddenly echoes through the room.

"*Start music?*"

All three of us jump.

"What just happened?" Lexi looks at Zora.

"I didn't do anything." Zora's cheeks flush red.

"You imitated her voice." My brain is suddenly working at full speed. "The escape room must think you're Red."

"*Start music?*" the robotic voice repeats.

I give Zora a firm nod.

"*Yes,*" Zora says in Red's throaty voice.

Immediately, a familiar melody fills the escape room. It's normally a cheerful tune, but now it sends chills down my spine.

Coming out of the loudspeakers is "Happy Birthday."

LEXI

"How did you do that?" Wide-eyed, I stare at Zora, who's turning redder and redder.

"Zora can imitate voices," says Beau. "She's crazy-good at it."

I look at Tess, who is gazing around in surprise. She can obviously hear the music too.

"Zora, try . . ." My eyes flash to the door.

Zora immediately gets what I mean and clears her throat. In Red's voice, she says: *"Open the door."*

The robotic voice doesn't respond.

"Open door."

But no matter what Zora tries, the robotic voice doesn't fall for it. When the song is over, the voice just asks if we'd like to start the music again.

"Please, no." Beau shakes his head. I know what he means: inside here, the tune has something sinister about it, as if we'll never have another birthday again.

I turn back to the glass and see Tess standing beside the last coffin. She's leaning over it and fiddling with the combination lock.

"What's she do—" In the middle of his sentence, Beau falls silent. We watch as Tess removes the lock and opens the lid.

"H-how . . . ?" stammers Beau.

"She got it open?" Zora joins us by the glass. "But how? We didn't get any clues, did we?"

"The song . . ." I hurry over to the coffin. "It's one of our birthdays!"

I immediately key in my own date: one, zero, two, five, and the lock opens. This lid is different than the others. It swings open on a hinge, like a blanket chest.

We swing it open without preparing ourselves. Because it can't get any worse than AJ and Kelly.

Shows how much we know.

When the lid is open, we see four photographs lined up inside the coffin.

Pictures of us.

CASE nr. 1999-5

E. Shepherd—psychiatrist

REPORT: AUDIO RECORDING

"I had no idea what would happen on
March thirteenth or I'd obviously
never have gone."

[Pause.]

"You need to know that her parents
are very strict. Particularly her
mother, who is always worried about
her. But we went anyway. To that
address on the business card. The
wind was howling. It was freezing
cold. And when we arrived, the other
two were already there. I didn't
know them, but my best friend did.
One of the two, at least. She liked

143

him. I could tell right away. She
practically swooned when he looked at
us. And then . . ."

She falls silent again. I wait
calmly.

"And then we went inside."

LEXI

"What's going on?" Beau pulls his own portrait out of the coffin. "This is my press pic."

I stare at mine, this year's school photo. Tess's picture was taken before the Shadow came. I was the one who took it, at the beach in the summer. She still had her red hair and almost as many freckles as me. Tess used it as her profile pic on the socials for months. Is that where Red got it from?

"*Hello.*" The robotic voice is back. "*Inside this coffin, there is room for only one of you. But which one will it be? Make a choice. Then say the name out loud, and the one you have chosen must get into the coffin and shut the lid. Complete this task and your time in the escape room will be over. Take note: the name that is spoken first will count.*"

Silence.

I try to process the information.

Coffin.

Photos.

One of us.

Zora is the first to say something.

"No. No way."

"Of course not." Beau throws his photo back into the coffin. "This is bullshit. No one's going to lie down in there!"

This is the end.

The escape room has a way out, but not for everyone.

The coffin is for one of us.

Who knows what's going to happen if we do this?

If Zora or Beau says my name now, I'll have to get into that coffin. Can I trust them? I've only known Zora for a few minutes! Beau seemed to be on my side, but that was only because we were a team. Now he's suddenly become my opponent.

And what if they name Tess?

I look at her on the other side of the glass. She's staring at the photos in her own coffin. Looks like she heard the message too. Would she be capable of sacrificing one of the others for the two of us?

But which one? Zora or Beau?

For a moment, I feel the warmth of his body again, close to me. I kissed him.

"We're not going to say anyone's name," says Beau. When I look up, my eyes meet his. "Got it?"

I nod slowly.

"If we say someone's name, it's all over for them."

Beau's eyes dart to Tess. "Make sure she keeps her mouth shut too, okay?"

I walk over to the glass and write two words: *no names*.

Tess doesn't look up. I knock pointlessly on the glass.

"Hey!" I shout, but I wonder if Tess would hear me even if I were standing right next to her. She's still staring at the photos in the coffin and seems to have completely forgotten about me.

"What should we do?" I hear Zora say.

"We wait," says Beau. "I'm sure people are going to start searching for us in a couple of hours. Those guys we met on the way here know where we are."

"The selfie guy!" Zora gasps. "You're right!"

"What are you doing now?" I whisper the words against the glass.

"Benji is going to lose it when he hears I'm missing," says Beau. "He'll get all my fans to help with the search."

"Don't do it," I say quietly to Tess. Maybe she'll hear me telepathically. We so often think and say the same thing at the same moment. Perhaps this is one of those moments. "Neither of them deserves to . . ."

What if Tess chooses Beau? A few hours ago I didn't even know him, but everything seems to have changed inside here. Sure, I still know hardly anything about him, but it's as if he's an important part of me, a part I'll never lose.

When I have nightmares about this escape room, I'll see *his* face in front of me. And I can never undo that kiss.

Whether I want it or not: Beau is in my system now.

I see Tess pick up a photo. Which of the two is it?

I wave my arms, but she's still not paying any attention to me. It's as if I'm behind a brick wall instead of a sheet of glass.

"That Red is going to be on the national news," I hear Zora say. "At least if we ever get out of here."

"We *are* going to get out!" Beau yells. "No one's dying in here, okay?"

"Guys?" I'm still looking at Tess.

They don't hear me.

"Guys!"

"What?" says Zora.

"I think she's going to choose someone."

"What?" Beau runs over to me, followed closely by Zora.

"What's she doing? Which photo is she holding? T—"

I clap my hand over Zora's mouth.

"Don't you dare say her name," I hiss. "You already abandoned her once. Do you want to do it again?"

"And what about us?" Zora yells between my fingers. "Is one of us going to have to pay the price for something we couldn't—"

At that moment Tess looks our way. When I see my cousin's dark eyes, I gasp and let go of Zora.

They're normally as green as leaves in springtime, but now they look black.

The Shadow is back.

"It's her own photo." Beau's voice is trembling. "She's holding her own photo!"

Tess's lips form a word I'd recognize anywhere.

She says her own name.

THIS
IS
THE
WAY
OUT

TESS

I know what people have been thinking about me. They don't have to say it. I can see it in the way they look at me. Like I'm made of glass. Not the kind in the escape room, but fragile glass. Like the glass animals in my grandma's display cabinet, which I was never allowed to touch.

Even people I've just met look at me that way. As if they can tell at a glance that I'm not one hundred percent participating in life. Like I'm just a walk-on extra, or some kind of stand-in.

The photos in the coffin grin at me, as if they're issuing a challenge. Zora with her perfect teeth, Beau with that captain's salute thing he always does in photo shoots. And, of course, Lexi.

Lexi, my twin cousin, born in the same week, just one day before me.

Sometimes I think all the happiness clung to her, so there was none left for me.

The medication is starting to wear off. I noticed a few minutes ago.

The spiders on the floor are back. I can see them crawling around my feet.

I know they're not real, but give it a couple of hours and I won't remember that.

The Shadow is slowly stirring within me. I don't have to fight it any longer.

I take a photo out of the coffin. Mine.

Lexi took it two summers ago. It's her favorite picture of me. She once said how happy I look in this photo, but I could hear what she really wanted to say: the Shadow wasn't there yet.

But is that true? Hasn't it always been there somewhere, waiting for a chance to strike? Maybe I was born with the Shadow.

I stroke my thumb over my summer freckles. I've never had as many as Lexi, but then again, she's completely covered with them.

When I look over my shoulder, I see her standing there. As pale as a corpse, but more beautiful than ever. She's always been the strong one of the two of us.

No names, she wrote on the glass.

Does she really think I'd do that to Zora or Beau?

Zora left me here on my own, but I don't hold that against her. Or when I realized she'd bought a clue and I had to pay the highest price. I wasn't even mad when the walls started coming in on me and I slit my side on something sharp. The walls only stopped moving when I started bleeding.

It was horrible, but I understand why Zora did it.

We all want to get out of here alive.

I glance again at the photo in my hand. I've been given a chance to put an end to this. Thanks to me, this escape room will finally be over. I hope Lexi understands that one day. That I did it for her. And even a bit for Beau and Zora.

They can still make a life for themselves outside of this place. That hasn't been true for me for a long time.

On the day Kelly jumped in front of the train, she took half of me with her.

And the other half filled up with black ink.

At the funeral, I heard everyone saying, *Why?*

But I understood perfectly why Kelly had done it. It was suddenly all I wanted too.

I take a deep breath and say my name: "Tess."

"Thank you for making your choice. Tess may take her place in the coffin."

On the other side of the glass, Lexi is feral. She's like a tiger at the zoo, jumping up and pawing the fence. Her red hair is swinging wildly around her face. I can't hear anything, but I can imagine how loud she's screaming now.

I tear my eyes away from the glass and turn back to the coffin. It has purple lining, like the first one.

Suddenly I think about Mom. I haven't thought about her since I got here. Maybe it was too hard.

But now that the moment has come, I suddenly see her with perfect clarity. Every morning, without fail, she asks me if I slept well. She lays out my pills on my breakfast plate, as if they're vitamins.

We've never really talked about it, but this must be horrible for her. Her daughter, her flesh and blood, slowly fading away.

I'm sure she'd have preferred a different daughter.

One like Lexi, full of energy.

I don't hold it against Lexi. I'm glad she can enjoy things so much. Like when she came up with the idea of this escape room.

Sometimes, through her, I can almost feel joy too.

Almost.

I place my hands on the edge of the coffin, which feels rough. I ignore the spider crawling over my hand and swing my leg over the edge.

The lining is even softer than it looks. As I lie down and take hold of the lid, it's as if all the medication drains out of my body at once.

The Shadow is back in full force.

But as long as I'm aware of that, I'm not too far gone, am I?

The tricky thing about the Shadow is that I don't

recognize it once it's fully there. The doctor explained it to me. As long as I can still analyze it, there's nothing to worry about. But when I can't do that anymore, I'm in big trouble.

There's another spider crawling over my arm.

It's here.

Lexi tried all these months to save me. It's time I did the same for her.

For my twin cousin.

I pull the lid shut in one movement. As soon as it's closed, the darkness is complete. My breath is racing, but there's barely any room to breathe. The lid is so close to my face. There's just an inch or so between my nose and the wood.

I need to stay calm, or I'll run out of oxygen.

Tess. Your best friend could not save you. Your name was spoken by another player, and now you are lying here. Thanks to that other player, you will soon be staring death in the face.

I let the words sink in, but they don't make sense. I said my own name, didn't I?

The voice continues, but I barely hear it. Another voice is forcing itself upon me, one I recognize immediately.

She's inside my head.

The voice that told me I had to go outside that night because it was dangerous inside.

She took me all the way to the highway.

She pointed out how beautiful the lights of the cars were.

She said heaven looked like that too.

Light.

My mom says the voice is dangerous. The doctor told us the medication would make her disappear.

But I don't know if I really mind her being here.

In a way, I'm glad she's back.

Fighting against it is more tiring than simply hearing her. Maybe I even missed her.

It's like finally getting to talk to an old friend you haven't seen for a while.

BEAU

"Tess!" Now Lexi is screaming her cousin's name. Not just once, but a hundred times. A thousand times. Louder and louder. She's banging on the glass as if she's trying to break through it, and the whole time she goes on screaming.

All I can do is watch. There's no way I'd dare touch her now.

"The door." Even before Zora says the word, I can feel what she means. There's a fresh wind coming into the room, and the light in here is changing.

When I look up, I see the metal door, the one Lexi and I made a dent in with the coffin lid. It's wide open.

The image is so ridiculous that I almost burst out laughing. Almost, because there's nothing to laugh about here.

"We're free." Zora looks at the door and then at me.

I look back at Lexi and then at the room opposite. The coffin Tess climbed into is just lying there, as if nothing had ever happened. But she must still be inside it. Does she have enough air? What's happening inside the coffin?

I run outside to the other team's door. I need to save Tess, as fast as I can.

But as soon as I step toward it, I see that the other door is still firmly closed. I try the handle, but it won't budge. When I pound against it with my shoulder, nothing happens.

"We need help!" I yell at Zora, who's joined me outside. "Go find someone!"

Zora starts running toward the main road.

I head back into the escape room, where Lexi is still thumping on the glass. She's screaming Tess's name over and over.

"Lexi . . . ," I say, tentatively approaching her. "Lexi, help is on its way. We're going to get Tess out of there."

Lexi looks up, her face covered in tears and snot. For a moment, I'm afraid she's going to slap me, as if I'm the one who put Tess inside the coffin, but then she wraps her arms around me really tight.

"Are you Beau?" A stranger jumps out of his car. On the passenger side, the door flies open and Zora gets out.

"You okay?" She comes over and sits down on Lexi's other side.

I'm sitting on the ground, just in front of the entrance,

with Lexi beside me. I'm still holding her hand, which I grabbed to guide her out of there. She had to get out of that place.

"Yes," I say.

"The police are coming!" The man runs up to us. "Are you guys okay?"

"There's someone else still in there." I feel Lexi freeze under my touch. "How long until the police get here?"

"A few minutes. At most. You guys want something to drink? To eat? Lisa, bring that bag over here!"

A girl who looks about twelve steps out of the car. She's staring at me wide-eyed, but I don't understand why at first.

The girl lugs over a big grocery bag, and the man takes it from her and starts digging around.

"Here," he says, holding out a bottle of soda, which I gratefully accept. I take a few big swigs and then hand it to Lexi.

She doesn't react, just goes on staring at the ground.

"Lexi," I say quietly. "Drink something. Please."

The man looks at Zora and then back at me. "When I saw her in front of my car, I thought she was a ghost. I only just braked in time! What the hell happened to you guys?"

There's a sound of sirens in the distance. Finally. The police. They'll get the door open. Tess will be rescued. If she just hangs on for a little longer . . .

161

The police car pulls up in front of the escape room, tires screeching. Zora starts yelling even before the officers are out of the car.

"Someone's still inside! A girl! Through that door there!"

One of the officers fetches a black metal tool from the car. I recognize it—a battering ram. You sometimes see cops in TV series using them to break down doors. It always seemed exciting, but now that I'm seeing it for real, it makes me want to vomit. With every thump of the battering ram, Lexi shrinks deeper and deeper into herself.

I hold her tighter and tighter. My fingertips are digging into her shoulder.

And then the door finally opens.

Lexi doesn't even react. She's completely in shock.

The voices of the two officers come from inside the building.

"Where's the girl?"

"In there?"

"No, try the other casket!"

More thumping. The sound of wood splintering.

"She's here! Whoa . . . What the . . . ? Is she still breathing? Where's that ambulance?!"

THIS
IS
TWO
MONTHS
LATER

BEAU

My eyes are fixed on the door. What's Lexi up to in there? She's been gone more than an hour and a half!

A girl on a bike is coming closer. I hang my head to hide my face, and she cycles past. Phew. But then she brakes. I see now that there's a second girl, riding on the back.

"Hey! I know you!" The girl jumps off the back of the bike. *"Oh my god! You're Beau!"*

The other girl drops her bike and the two of them come running up to me.

"Can we get a picture with you?"

Without waiting for my reply, she takes out her phone.

Why didn't I wear a baseball cap this morning? I don't want more new photos on social media right now. Not when people are finally starting to forget those pictures at the police station.

"Hey, Beau. How are you doing?" The girl sits down

beside me, tossing her long hair over one shoulder. It sweeps across my cheek.

"Yeah, how are you now?" The second girl takes the photo and then swaps places with her friend. "You know, I really think you should make a song about it."

I look at her. "Sorry?"

"Like, about what it was like for you in that escape room. I think it could be really cool."

I try to come up with an answer, but I draw a blank. My tongue suddenly seems to be made of clay.

"Just as a bonus track. That should work now that your new album's been delayed, right?"

I think about Benji, who came to the police station as soon as he heard what had happened. His eyes were red and he was dripping with sweat. He kept saying over and over how sorry he was, that I didn't need to worry about the press, that he'd take care of everything. To my surprise, he even postponed our trip to LA. He said the people from the label would understand.

We haven't even talked about the tour. Every day I expect a message from him, but he's leaving me alone, just like he promised.

The fans aren't, though. They're everywhere, all the time.

"Give me a smile, hey?" The girl nudges me. "Then she can take a photo of us."

I stare at the phone in front of me. I manage to squeeze out a smile, but I'm sure it looks more like a grimace.

I'd really like to run away, but I promised to wait here for Lexi. I always do that on Wednesday afternoons, and then we usually go into town together.

As soon as the girls are gone, I hear the door open behind me. I turn and see Lexi, and she beams when she spots me. I don't; I must look like a ghost.

"You're here already." Lexi throws her arms around me, and I close my eyes for a moment.

"How was it?" I mumble into her hair.

"That Shepherd guy asks some really annoying questions, but he's good." Lexi lets go of me. "You sure you don't want to talk to him sometime? He has a spot free on Friday, so . . ."

"Yeah, I'm sure."

No way I'm digging everything up again. Lexi told me about the EMDR therapy, but it sounds like magical thinking. How can something like that really work?

"Want to get a coffee somewhere?" I ask to distract her.

Lexi nods. "Okay. But first, there's somewhere I want to take you."

"A surprise?"

"Well, not really a surprise." Lexi suddenly looks serious. "It's something else. Come on." She takes hold of my hand. It's addictively good, the casual way she just does it.

She doesn't seem to care what anyone else thinks. Some fans took photos of us the other day, but she didn't seem bothered by that either.

Just let them, she says. *We know what's what, don't we?*

But that's the problem: I don't know what's what. I have no idea where the two of us stand, whether she likes me or if she's just grateful that I was her teammate in there.

Since that kiss between the four concrete walls, not much has changed.

The only thing that *has* changed is that we spend so much time together. Lexi's been to my place for dinner five times now. My mom and dad are crazy about her. And I know my way around her house too.

Zora jokes that we're like a married couple. But we haven't done anything more than hold hands.

Lexi and I walk past the venue where I had my last performance. As we pass the alleyway behind it, I see Red in my mind again. They still haven't tracked her down. The sketch based on our descriptions doesn't look much like the woman who spoke to me here, but I couldn't say what needs to be changed.

Red is fading away, like a Polaroid in reverse.

I'm sure it won't be much longer before the police stop searching for her. Other cases will take priority.

We cross the bridge and head into the busiest part of town. I have no idea what Lexi's planning.

"We're almost there," she says, turning left.

My body recognizes the place before my brain does. It's like something starts crackling and fizzing inside my head, like popping candy.

"What are we doing here?" My voice sounds as heavy as lead.

Lexi comes to a stop on the sidewalk. "It was here, wasn't it?"

The intersection is even busier than I remember. Cars are racing past. The cyclists and pedestrians all seem to be in a hurry.

I stare at the spot. It's like nothing ever happened here. Even the flowers and the photo have been taken away.

"How . . . ?" My head is thumping. "How do you know about this?"

"I looked you up," Lexi admits with a grin. "It's true. You *are* actually pretty famous."

"You did *what*?"

"Sorry." Lexi smiles. "But I wanted to find out why you didn't know anything about . . . Kelly."

When she says the name, her voice falters.

"You told me a while ago that you were really busy around that time, so I wanted to see what you were up to. But you didn't do anything at all from October to January. You completely disappeared from the radar. All your fans were talking about it."

"I . . . I was working on songs for the new album."

"So I went on looking." Lexi ignores my lie. "I found an

article about an accident in September, just before Kelly. It was here, at this spot, right by the studio. Your name was mentioned in passing. So you were there?"

My mouth is dry.

When I don't reply, Lexi continues: "I read that an eleven-year-old got hit by a car at this intersection. And that she died."

I want Lexi to stop talking. Right now.

"Stop," I say.

"Why do you feel guilty?"

"What do you mean?"

"Don't lie to me, Beau. I know guilt when I see it. Better than anyone." Lexi's expression becomes serious. "So why?"

Another car races past.

"Because it *was* my fault."

Lexi shakes her head. "You weren't in the car, were you?"

"Like the article said, I was here." I point at the spot where we're standing now. "I got recognized."

"By the girl?"

I shake my head. "By the driver."

It's like I hear Mariposa's scream all over again. The screeching brakes, the dull thud. And then the silence.

"And what happened?"

"The woman at the wheel called my name, said her daughter was a huge fan. I shouted back at her to say hi

170

from me. She drove off, smiling. She wasn't paying attention as she turned the corner. So she just . . . drove straight
over the girl."

Again, I see the casket. The white one with blue butterflies. Butterflies, because of her name.

Lexi looks at me as if she's waiting for the rest of the
story. But there is no rest of the story.

"Bullshit," she says.

"Sorry?"

"It's horrible, what happened to that girl, but there's
absolutely nothing you could do about it."

"I was there, and I got recognized," I say. Wasn't Lexi
listening?

"Please!" Lexi runs her hands through her hair. "You
need to stop being so self-important!"

"Sorry?" My hands are tingling.

"That woman could just as easily have been saying
hello to her hairdresser or to another mother from school!"

"But—"

"No." Now Lexi takes hold of both my hands. She's
quite a bit shorter than me, but it feels like we're on the
same level.

"You were here, but that's all."

"You have no idea what it did to Mariposa's family. It
destroyed them," I say quietly. "At the memorial service,
her mom was just about drowning in tears."

"You went to the memorial service?" Lexi exclaims.

"Yeah. I kept my distance, though. I didn't introduce myself to anyone. I just wanted to . . ."

"To punish yourself," says Lexi.

I nod slowly. "Something like that."

"You've been punished enough." Lexi squeezes my right hand and then my left one. "Please go talk to Shepherd. About the girl, about the escape room, about everything."

"The man's not some kind of miracle worker," I say.

"He pretty much is." Lexi lets go of my hands, and they fall by my sides. "He even got Tess talking."

LEXI

For the first time in weeks, I say her name again. It still feels bad, like saying her name takes me back into the escape room. Since we escaped, I've abbreviated our names: T, B, and Zor.

"How's she doing now?" Beau looks at me with a worried expression. That's how he looks a lot of the time since we escaped. He means well, but I miss the annoying grin he had when we first met.

"Better," I say. "The new medication is working. She says she doesn't see spiders anymore."

I think back to my last visit with Tess. For the first time, I felt like I saw a glimpse of the old Tess.

"My aunt says they might let her come home between therapy sessions soon."

I know Tess can't wait. She hates the clinical atmosphere at the hospital. She said the other day that it feels like another escape room, with all those closed doors.

"Has she . . ." Beau hesitates. "Has she told Shepherd anything about the minutes she spent inside the coffin?"

I see Tess climbing into the coffin again. That's the moment I chose for the EMDR. Shepherd told me to focus on the most traumatic part of the memory, and that was the image that immediately came to mind.

I can still see it all so clearly. I can still make out every detail, but the anxiety is a lot less intense. As if there's a veil over the memory.

Beau doesn't want anything to do with EMDR, but I think it works like magic. After every session with Shepherd, I feel lighter.

"I don't know, but I hope so," I say. "Talking really helps."

Beau sighs. "You sound almost like a psychiatrist yourself."

"Who knows? Maybe I will be a psychiatrist one day. You still want to go for that coffee? I know a nice place above a bookstore."

We walk on together. A group of girls on the other side of the street starts screaming and pointing. I feel Beau tense up beside me.

"Just let them have some fun," I say. "They're happy to see you."

"I didn't say anything, did I?" Beau stares sullenly ahead. Zora and I have tried everything, but that frown has barely left his face since the escape room. It's like he's still inside the room, not physically, but in his mind.

"When are you going to LA?" I say, glancing at him. "That deal won't be on offer forever."

Beau shrugs. It's exactly like Zora said. He seems to want to completely forget about his career. It was weeks before he even told us about LA. Like he didn't think it was important.

"Or we could go stand by the railroad tracks," I say. "If you want to feel something again."

"What the . . . ?" Beau stops walking. "What's that supposed to mean?"

"You're ruining everything," I say. "Is that what you want?"

"Ruining everything? How? I swear I'm going to start singing again eventually," he says, blushing. "I'll go on tour, have my photo taken, do meet-and-greets, smile when I'm expected to smile, I'll—"

"Don't be so pathetic."

Beau looks so stunned that I almost burst out laughing.

"I mean it," I continue. "You're not the only one who was in that escape room. Zor and I were terrified the whole time too, not to mention Tess."

My throat feels tight, but I refuse to cry.

"The three of us are doing everything we can to get better, to move on, but what are *you* doing? Singing is your life!"

"Yeah? How do you know that?"

"I looked you up. Remember?" I think about the video

that appeared at the top of the feed: Beau throwing up onstage. I didn't click on that one. I chose a performance at an amusement park, from last summer. The girl who filmed it was standing right at the front and she recorded the whole thing.

It felt strange to see Beau like that, through the eyes of a fan.

"You were singing your first single. It was perfect. I felt so proud when I saw you."

"Because I'm famous?"

"Because you seemed happy!" I stifle the urge to give him a good shake. "I don't care if you have a thousand fans or just one. But if you go on like this, you really *are* going to end up with just one fan."

Beau raises his eyebrows.

"Benji," I add. "Because you're driving me and Zor crazy."

"You and Zora?" Beau asks.

"Yes." I stand up straight. "We do sometimes meet up without you. Girls' stuff, you know."

"Zora hates girls' stuff."

"Apparently not." I quickly walk on, along the busy shopping street. I can see the sign for the bookstore in the distance.

When we're standing in front of the display window, Beau takes my hand. "Hang on a second."

"What?"

"You're right. Okay?" Beau's eyes dart back and forth. He hardly dares to look at me. "I know I'm messing things up. With my fans, with Benji, with Zora, with you . . ."

I look at his fingers for a moment, intertwined with mine. We often walk hand in hand, but it's always me who takes the initiative. It's like Beau doesn't dare.

This arrogant pop star, who has half the country at his feet, doesn't even dare to take my hand. Let alone kiss me.

"I'm going to try harder." Beau's eyes finally come to rest. "I'll talk to Shepherd."

I look at him in surprise. "Really?"

"Don't be so enthusiastic. If I don't like it, I'm out of there."

A girl who looks about nine years old approaches us and taps Beau on the back.

"Are you Beau?" she asks.

"Um . . . Yes."

"Can I have your autograph?"

"Sure." Beau takes a pen out of his pocket and writes his name on the girl's arm.

"Thank you." The girl beams at Beau. "I'm never going to wash it again!"

She runs back to her mom and dad. Beau clicks the top back onto the pen.

"Was that so hard?" I say. "A little bit of friendliness

and you've made her whole day. How about that? I mean, it's amazing that you can achieve something like that just by—"

In the middle of my sentence, Beau leans forward and presses his lips to mine. On a crowded shopping street, without concrete walls around us. I feel his warm body against mine, and his left hand finds my right hand now too.

When he moves his face away from mine, I feel my cheeks burning. They're just about on fire.

"What?" he says. "No smart comments this time?"

"Not yet," I say. "But give me a moment."

Smiling, Beau pulls me into the bookstore. "So, where are we going?"

"Upstairs."

Then the two of us stop in our tracks. The elevator in front of us is mostly made of glass, but I still feel my heart pounding painfully. For a second, I'm back inside the escape room. We plummeted, shot back up, fell again. I thought it was never going to stop.

My hands are getting clammy.

"Hey," the voice beside me says. When I look up, Beau's grin has finally returned. The tension slowly starts to slide out of my body, like during an EMDR session.

"Why don't we take the stairs?"

CASE nr. 1999-5

E. Shepherd—psychiatrist

REPORT: AUDIO RECORDING

"That bunker dated back to the Cold
War. That's what Marjon said, anyway.
I wanted to find out all about it,
but she was only interested in the
two guys. Particularly the tall one:
Danny. He liked her. I could see that
immediately. And she was into him.
She was raised really strictly, you
know? So she'd never had a boyfriend
before."

She glances away. Seems to be in a
completely different world. Then she
goes on with her story.

"It stank inside the bunker. There

were empty beer cans and scraps of
food all over the place. I think a
lot of bums used to hang out there.
That Danny guy took a tin out of his
pocket and gave us this mysterious
look. He said he had some weed and
asked if we wanted to try. Marjon
immediately said yes, of course.
When I hesitated, she laughed. She
told them I'd tried smoking once and
couldn't stop coughing. And said that
weed wasn't my kind of thing. Like
she had loads of experience! But
whatever . . ."

There's another silence. She's
clearly bothered by this part about
her best friend, Marjon.

"The three of them smoked a joint
while I just stood there. We walked
on for a bit. The bunker was like a
maze. There were so many corridors!
The three of them were getting
sillier and sillier. Marjon kept
giggling at everything that Danny guy
said. I said her mom and dad would
kill her if they found out, but that
just made her laugh too.

"And then they started kissing. Right in front of me. I didn't know where to look, especially when Danny put his hands under her T-shirt. The other guy looked at me and asked if I wanted to do the same with him.

"In his dreams! I said I wanted to leave, but Marjon got mad. She said I always ruined everything."

She swallows.

"Suddenly there was all this noise, like things being knocked over. There was someone else in there, not far from us. We were scared to death, and Danny and Marjon immediately ran away. Danny had the flashlight with him. I could see the beam of light darting back and forth with every step he took. His friend went after them, but I couldn't keep up. I was falling more and more behind, so I yelled at them to wait. But they didn't."

Now she takes a tissue, but she holds it in her hands.

"I lost them."

She rips a corner off the tissue.

"Within a few seconds, I was alone in the darkness. And it was *so* dark. Not like in a theater just before the movie begins, but completely black. I couldn't see a thing. I tried walking on, but I kept bumping into the walls. Every time I found a way through, there were more walls. I screamed at them to come back, but they didn't."

The tissue is in three pieces on her lap now, and she just keeps on tearing away.

"And where was the person we'd run away from? What kind of person was wandering around a bunker? And what would they do if they found me? I wanted to run, but I tripped and fell hard. My leg was broken, and I couldn't walk more than a few steps on it at a time. The earth was damp and ice-cold. I was wearing a winter coat, but it didn't feel like it. Soon I was shivering nonstop."

I have to force myself not to ask any questions at this point, but

I promised not to interrupt her story.

"My mom and dad were so worried when I didn't come home that night. They obviously checked at Marjon's first, but she just said I'd gone home, like she had.

"So my mom and dad reported me missing to the police, and they started a search.

"The police didn't find anything, because they didn't know about the bunker. Marjon had left out that part. She was too chicken to say where we'd really been. And she kept silent about the boys, because she was way too scared of her mom and dad. If she told them about the bunker, it would come out that we hadn't been there on our own. Then she'd have to tell them about Danny and the weed. . . .

"Do you know how long it took my best friend to open her mouth? A day and a half!

"It took her a whole day and a

half before she dared to tell anyone
where we'd been!

"The police started a search of the
bunkers and they finally found me."

I notice that she's skipped the
most important part. She didn't say
anything about the day and a half
when she was in there alone, but I
can imagine what it must have been
like.

"I saw Marjon not so long ago,
just the one time. She was nervous.
There were red blotches on her
throat. She never said sorry. Never."

There are only shreds of the
tissue left now.

"I don't trust anyone anymore.
Obviously. Because if your best
friend can leave you to rot for a day
and a half, then who can you trust?"

She looks away and stares outside.

"A few days ago, I was by the sea.
I wondered how it would feel just to
disappear into the water. Then the
nightmares would finally stop."

"Death is never the solution."

She looks up, irritated. For a

moment, I'm afraid she'll get up and leave because I broke my promise, but then she sighs.

"Perhaps not. But neither is your EMDR."

"We could maybe give it another try?"

"No, thank you." She stands up.

"Where are you going?"

"That was my story. I'm done."

"But—"

"Now you can close the file." She's already standing at the door. "See you never, Mr. Shepherd."

RED

From here, I have a perfect view of Shepherd's office. In all these years, hardly anything has changed. Even the hideous sculpture on the windowsill is still there.

He's sitting behind the lace curtain. I can picture him right now. Gray at the temples, a well-trimmed beard, and always in a shirt and dress pants.

He'll be completely gray by now, but I'm sure that otherwise he looks exactly the same as he did in 1999, when I first met him.

He was invited to be a consultant for the Escape Room 2.0 case. Did he think about me then? Did he see the similarities with the case in 1999? Maybe I shouldn't have added the "best friends competing against each other" aspect. It could easily have given me away.

But at the same time it's what makes my escape room so special. Inside Escape Room 2.0, you find out who your real friends are. And if they'll stand by your side or ultimately betray you to save their own skin.

It was a gamble, putting those four photos in the last coffin. Beau and Lexi could have chosen someone else, after all. But having observed them for weeks, I knew they wouldn't.

Simply because they had no alternative.

They were perfect.

Lexi and Beau barely remembered what I looked like. Luckily, the sketch the police artist did of me wasn't even close. There's no way Shepherd could have recognized me from that. Even so, to be on the safe side, I changed my appearance. I'm not wearing red anymore.

Red. How did they come up with that?

I look at the front door again. The last time I went to Shepherd, I told him my story. It didn't make me feel any better, though. Of course it didn't.

Talking doesn't help.

EMDR doesn't help.

But he's still doing his little trick. He's really convinced that it works.

I was one of his first guinea pigs in 1999, when it was still pretty much unknown.

But it didn't work. Quite the opposite. Ever since then, the images in my head have just become more vivid. As if I'm constantly living in that moment.

Alone in the bunker.

In the darkness.

Without any sense of time.

Afraid that I'm never going to be found . . .

A boy with dark curls is standing by Shepherd's door now. He's hanging his head, as if he's trying to make himself invisible.

He looked like that when I first met him too.

Even when two girls talk to him and take photos with him, his posture barely changes.

The girls happily cycle off again, and the boy is alone.

Beau.

My favorite player of the four. Arrogant and sweet. Predictable and surprising. All at the same time.

I wasn't able to watch them in there, but I heard everything.

And from the building across the street I had a perfect view of their escape. When Beau dragged Lexi out of that escape room, he was like a hero. He didn't have to do it, but he stayed with her. Even in the police car, he sat beside her, like a kind of bodyguard.

Now Shepherd's door finally opens. Lexi throws her arms around Beau. Lexi, the girl who stood by the tracks every Thursday night until I came along. She reminded me of myself.

But neither of us did what AJ Loper and Kelly Kleefman did.

I had to change Lexi's mind. There are too many suicides in this country. Particularly among young people, who are the same age as I was then.

Shepherd can't help them.

But I can.

I can show them who their friends are.

Who they can trust and who they can't.

I save them. Like a lifeguard. Maybe that was why I chose to wear red.

I watch Beau and Lexi walking away together, hand in hand.

Since my escape room, Lexi hasn't stood by the railroad track again.

And Beau finally has someone who sees him as he *really* is.

Thanks to me, the two of them found each other.

But they didn't just find each other: they found Life.

I gave that back to them.

Tess was a mistake. If I'd known the girl had mental health problems, I'd never have agreed to her participation.

But I'm allowed to make mistakes, aren't I? This was only my first attempt.

EMDR was obviously not an instant hit either.

You have to keep working at that kind of thing, polishing it.

Now that my inheritance from my mom and dad has almost run out, I'm going to have to get even more creative. I hope I can find another good, reliable construction company and technicians, because I'll never manage to put something like that together by myself.

I turn and head in the opposite direction.

I can't use the location on Industry Road anymore. They'll be looking for me there.

I'll have to find a new place, so I have my work cut out for me.

But now I know what I'm doing it for.

There are plenty more young people out there who need my help.

THIS
IS
WHERE
THE
AUTHOR
TALKS

If you're struggling, don't keep it to yourself. Talking helps. So reach out to someone. Sooner rather than later!

Call 988 to speak with a trained counselor.

ACKNOWLEDGMENTS

Escape Room was my first YA thriller, and it still has a lot of readers. When I visit schools, students often ask me if I'd like to write another book about an escape room. Seems my readers aren't done with this concept yet!

I decided if I was going to write a new book about an escape room, it had to be original. Different from the first, maybe even scarier . . .

No Escape began to take shape in my head, and I started writing.

The first idea that came to mind was to explore EMDR (eye movement desensitization and reprocessing) therapy. I only know people for whom it worked really well, but their stories made me wonder: What if it didn't turn out so well? Might someone then come up with their own form of therapy and create an escape room for young people that was designed to wake them up to "reality"?

Thanks for all the many requests for an *Escape Room* 2.0. Without you, this book would never have happened.